D0229983

LIBRARIES NI
WITHDRAWN FROM STOCK

"I bet if you tried you could find something you like about me. Maybe this will help."

Mark wrapped an arm around her waist and pulled her to him. Laura Jo only had time to gasp before his lips found hers. She didn't react at first, which gave him time to taste her lips. Soft, warm and slightly parted. Then for the briefest of seconds she returned his kiss. His heart thumped against his ribs at the possibilities before her hands spread wide against his chest. She shoved him away— hard.

His hands fell to his sides.

"You had no right to do that," she breathed.

"I can't say that I'm sorry."

She slid behind the steering wheel, and before she could close the door he said, "Goodnight, Laura Jo."

"It's more like goodbye." She slammed the door.

Not a chance. Mark watched her taillights disappear up his drive. They'd be seeing each other again if he had anything to say about it. She was the first woman he'd met who had him thinking about the possibilities of tomorrow, even when he shouldn't.

Dear Reader,

For years I have been fascinated with the concept of Mardi Gras and the tradition behind it. Most people only know of wild, free-spirited times in New Orleans. When Kathy Cooksey, a friend of mine, moved to Louisiana I learned that there is more to the season than what I've seen on TV. During a visit to her house my children and I enjoyed a family atmosphere of parades and King Cake. Boy, did we attend parades! Sometimes as many as three a day. Even my youngest would holler, 'Hey, mister, throw me some beads!'

I later learned that Mobile, Alabama, was the first city in America to celebrate Mardi Gras. At the Mardi Gras Museum located there I discovered the behind-the-scenes events of the local society. I learned about krewes. Another friend and I attended one of the balls, and had the pleasure of seeing the King and Queen along with their court—which I describe in the book.

Laura Jo and Mark's story takes place during the Mardi Gras season. As medical personnel they help, but they also get in on the fun. It is a time of high revelry and—for them—a chance for change. Mardi Gras is about living high and then giving something up for Lent. As you read Laura Jo and Mark's story you will see that they did just that and found life all the better. I hope you enjoy their story and the Mardi Gras season surrounding it.

If you would like to make your own King Cake and gumbo you can find the recipes on my website at SusanCarlisle.com. I also love to hear from my readers.

Susan

THE DOCTOR'S REDEMPTION

BY
SUSAN CARLISLE

LIBRARIES NI	
C901392742	
MAG	12.02.16
AF	£14.99
AHS	

of the publisher in any form of binding or cover other than that in which it is published and without a similar condition including this condition being imposed on the subsequent purchaser.

® and TM are trademarks owned and used by the trademark owner and/or its licensee. Trademarks marked with ® are registered with the United Kingdom Patent Office and/or the Office for Harmonisation in the Internal Market and in other countries.

First published in Great Britain 2015
by Mills & Boon, an imprint of Harlequin (UK) Limited,
Large Print edition 2015
Eton House, 18-24 Paradise Road,
Richmond, Surrey, TW9 1SR

© 2015 Susan Carlisle

ISBN: 978-0-263-25507-2

Harlequin (UK) Limited's policy is to use papers that are natural, renewable and recyclable products and made from wood grown in sustainable forests. The logging and manufacturing processes conform to the legal environmental regulations of the country of origin.

Printed and bound in Great Britain
by CPI Antony Rowe, Chippenham, Wiltshire

Susan Carlisle's love affair with books began when she made a bad grade in maths in the sixth grade. Not allowed to watch TV until she'd brought the grade up, she filled her time with books and became a voracious romance reader. She still has 'keepers' on the shelf to prove it. Because she loved the genre so much she decided to try her hand at creating her own romantic worlds. She still loves a good happily-ever-after story.

When not writing Susan doubles as a high school substitute teacher, which she has been doing for sixteen years. Susan lives in Georgia with her husband of twenty-eight years and has four grown children. She loves castles, travelling, cross-stitching, hats, James Bond and hearing from her readers.

Books by Susan Carlisle

The Maverick Who Ruled Her Heart
The Doctor Who Made Her Love Again
Snowbound with Dr Delectable
NYC Angels: The Wallflower's Secret
Hot-Shot Doc Comes to Town
The Nurse He Shouldn't Notice
Heart Surgeon, Hero...Husband?

**Visit the author profile page at
millsandboon.co.uk for more titles**

To Kathy Cooksey and Jeanie Brantley.
Thanks for sharing Mardi Gras with me.

Praise for Susan Carlisle

'Shimmering with breathtaking romance amid the medical drama, spectacular emotional punch, a believable conflict and vivid atmospheric details, *NYC Angels: The Wallflower's Secret* is sure to thrill Medical Romance readers.'
—*GoodReads*

CHAPTER ONE

THE PARADES WERE what Laura Jo Akins enjoyed most about the Mardi Gras season in Mobile, Alabama. This year was no different. She placed a hand on the thin shoulder of her eight-year-old daughter, Allie.

Her daughter smiled up at her. "When does the parade start?"

"It should already be moving our way. Listen. You can hear the band."

The faint sound of a ragtime tune floated from the distance.

Allie looked up at Laura Jo. "Can we stay for the next one too?"

The sure thing about Mardi Gras was that the parades kept coming. The closer the calendar got to Fat Tuesday the more heavily the days were filled with parades. Sometimes as many as four a day on the weekends.

"No, honey. They're expecting me at the hospital. We'll watch this one and then we have to go."

"Okay, but we get to see one another day, don't we?"

"Maybe on Wednesday. Next Monday and Tuesday you'll be out of school for a long weekend. We'll be sure to watch more then."

"Why can't I be in one?" Allie asked, turning to look at Laura Jo.

It had been a constant question during last year's Mardi Gras season and had become more demanding during this one. "Maybe when you get older. For now we'll just have to watch."

As the banner holders at the head of the parade came into sight the crowd pushed forward, forcing her and Allie against the metal barriers. A bicycling medical first responder or mobile EMT circled in front of them then rode up the street. He looked familiar for some reason but, then, most of the medical help during the carnival season were employed at the hospital where she worked. Dressed in red biking shorts and wearing a pack on his back, he turned again and pedaled back in their direction. Laura Jo squinted, trying to make out his features, but his helmet obscured her view.

Members of the medical community volunteered to work during Mardi Gras to help out with the crowds. Most of the nurses and doctors gave up their days off during the season to work the parades. It wasn't required but many enjoyed being a part of the celebration. Laura Jo knew most of the employees at Mobile General, at least by face. Although she couldn't place the rider, he looked just fine in his formfitting pants. He must bike regularly.

"Look, Mommy." Allie pointed to a group of people who had come through the barriers and were entertaining the crowd standing on both sides of the street. They were dressed in clown-type outfits and were riding three-wheeled bikes with bright-colored fish attached to the side.

Laura Jo smiled down at her daughter. "That's the Mystic Fish."

They made a circle or two in the open parade area and then disappeared into the crowd across the street from her and Allie. Laura Jo knew from years of watching parades that they would appear somewhere else along the parade route.

"What's a mystic fish?" Allie asked.

"You know what a fish is. In this case it's a club or group of people. It's also called a krewe. Because they meet in secret they are mystic or mysterious. It's all just fun."

"Are you in a queue?'

"It's krewe. Like a crew member. And, no, I'm not." She placed a hand on her daughter's head. "I have you to take care of, work at the shelter and at the hospital. No time."

Laura Jo understood being a member of a krewe. Her family had been participants all her life. In fact, they had been a part of the largest and most prestigious krewe in Mobile. She'd been one of the Mobile society that had celebrated her coming of age at carnival time. But no more.

The noise level increased as the first high-school band approached. She positioned Allie between her and the barrier so Allie could see. As the first ostentatiously decorated float rolled by the spectators pressed closer to them. The float was designed in a dragon motif and painted green, purple and gold with piles of beads hanging off pegs. Members of the krewe were dressed in costumes and wore masks.

She and Allie joined those around them in yelling, "Throw me something, mister."

Raising their hands along with everyone else, she and Allie tried to catch the beads, plastic cups with the krewe name printed on them or stuffed animals that were being thrown from the float. Bands playing and music blaring from large speakers mounted on the floats made it difficult to hear.

One krewe member made eye contact with Laura Jo and pointed at Allie. He threw a small stuffed gorilla to Laura Jo, which she handed to Allie, who hugged it to her and smiled up at the grinning man. The float moved on.

When a strand of brightly colored beads flew through the air in Allie's direction from the next float, Laura Jo reached to catch them. She couldn't and they were snatched by the man standing behind her. He handed them to Allie. She smiled brightly at him. That was one of the special things about Mardi Gras in Mobile. It was a family affair. Any age was welcome and everyone saw that the children had a good time. Twenty minutes later a fire truck that signaled the end of the parade rolled by.

The man standing next to them shifted the barrier, creating an opening. A few people rushed through in an effort to snatch up any of the goodies that had fallen on the pavement.

"Mama, can I get those?" Allie pointed out into the street, now virtually empty except for a few children.

Laura Jo searched for what Allie was asking about. On the road lay a couple of plastic doubloons. "Sure, honey. There won't be another parade for an hour."

Allie ran through the opening and ran in the direction of the strand of gold and silver disks. In her exuberance to reach her target she stumbled and fell, stopping herself with her hands. Laura Jo gasped and rushed to her. Allie had already pushed herself up to a sitting position. Tears welled in her eyes but she'd not burst into sobs yet. There was an L-shaped hole in the thin material of her pants and a trickle of blood ran off the side of her knee.

"Oh, honey," Laura Jo said.

"My hands hurt." Allie showed Laura Jo her palms. The meaty part looked much like her knee.

"Friction burns." Laura Jo took one of Allie's

wrists and raised her hand, blowing across it. Here she was a registered nurse with not a bandage to her name. Allie's injuries were going to require far more than what Laura Jo was doing.

"Can I help here?" a deep male voice said from above them.

Laura Jo glanced up to see the bike medic she'd admired earlier. She'd been so adsorbed with Allie she'd not noticed him ride up.

"Do you have any four-by-fours? Some antibiotic cream?" Laura Jo asked.

The man gave her a curious look then stepped off the bike. He slung the red pack off his back and crouched down on his haunches. "Let me see what I can do."

Laura Jo looked at him through moisture in her eyes. She knew him. Or more accurately knew who he was. Mark Clayborn. She'd had no idea he was back in town. But, then, why would she? "If you'll just share your supplies I can handle it. I'm her mother and a nurse."

"I appreciate that but I need to treat your daughter since it happened at the parade. I'll have to make a report anyway."

She gave him room. Years ago she'd been very

enamored of Mark Clayborn. Just young enough to hero worship him, she'd often dreamed of "what if" when he'd glanced her way. Which he never had, unless it had been to smile at the gaggle of young maids in his queen's court. He'd had it all. Good looks, social status, education and a bright future. And to top it off he'd been Mardi Gras King that year. Every girl had dreamed of being on his arm and she'd been no different. She had watched him so closely back then no wonder he seemed familiar.

Allie winced when he touched the angry skin of her knee.

Laura Jo's hands shook. As an emergency room nurse she'd seen much worse, but when it came to her own child it was difficult to remain emotionally detached. Still, she should be the one caring for Allie. She'd been her sole caretaker and provider since her daughter's father had left Laura Jo when she was three months pregnant. Having been pushed aside before, she didn't like it any better now than she had then. No matter how irrational the reaction.

"So what's your name, young lady?" Mark asked Allie.

She told him.

"So, Allie, what have you liked best about Mardi Gras this year?"

Allie didn't hesitate to answer. "King Cake."

He nodded like a sage monk giving thought to the answer. "I like King Cake, too. What's your favorite? Cinnamon or cream cheese?"

"Cinnamon."

"I'm a fan of cream cheese. So have you ever found the baby?"

"Yeah, once. I had to take a cake to school the next week."

"So you baked one?"

"No, my mother did." She pointed at Laura Jo.

Mark glanced at her with a look of respect but there was no sign of recognition. Even though their families had known each other for years he didn't remember her. The last she'd really heard, he'd been in a bad car accident and had later left for medical school.

"You mom didn't get it from a bakery?"

"No. She likes to make them." Allie smiled up at Laura Jo. "She lets me put the baby inside."

Allie continued, telling him how she liked to stand beside Laura Jo as she rolled the pastry out.

She would wait patiently until it was time to put the miniature plastic baby into one of the rolls before Laura Jo braided them into a cake. When it came out of the oven Allie begged to be the one to shake the green, purple and gold sugar on top.

"Well, that sounds like fun. Are you ready to stand?"

Laura Jo couldn't help but be impressed. Mark had cleaned up Allie with little more than a wince from her.

He placed a hand below Allie's elbow and helped her to stand then said to Laura Jo, "Keep the area clean. If you see any infection, call a doctor right away or take her to the ER."

Laura Jo rolled her eyes. "I'm a nurse, remember?"

"I remember, but sometimes when it's someone we love our emotions get in the way."

That was something close to what her father had said when she'd announced that she was marrying Phil. "He's only interested in your last name and money." Her father had gone on to say that Phil certainly wasn't worth giving up her education for. When she'd asked how her father knew so much about Phil he admitted to having had someone check into his background. That Phil had already been married once and couldn't seem to hold down a job. "He's not good enough for you. Not welcome in our home," had been her father's parting words.

She'd chosen Phil. Even though she'd soon learned that her father had been right, the situation had created a rift between Laura Jo and her parents that was just as wide today as it had been nine years earlier. She had sworn then never to ask her parents for help. She had her pride.

Taking Allie's hand, Laura Jo said, "Let's go, honey. I'm sure we have taken enough of the medic's time."

"Bye," Allie said.

Mark bent and picked up the doubloons off the pavement and placed them carefully in Allie's hand. "I hope you find a baby in your next cake. Maybe it'll bring you luck."

Allie grinned back at him with obvious hero worship.

"Thank you." She led Allie through the barrier. "Bye."

That would be it for the reappearing Mark Clayborn. He had been a part of her life that was now long gone. She wouldn't be seeing him again.

Mark had never planned to return to Mobile to live permanently, but that had changed. He'd worked hard to make LA home. Even the few times he'd come back to Alabama he'd only stayed a few days and then gone again. When his father's houseman had phoned to say Mark Clayborn, Sr. had suffered a stroke, Mark could no longer refuse not to make southern Alabama his home again. His mother was gone and his brother was in the military with no control over where he was stationed. Mark was left no choice. Someone needed to live close enough to take care of his father.

Pulling up the circular drive framed by a well-manicured yard in the center of the oldest section of homes in Mobile, Mark stopped in front of the antebellum mansion. This house had been his home for the twenty-five years before he had moved to LA. Now just his father lived here. Mark had chosen to take up residence forty-five minutes across the bay in the Clayborn summer house in Fairhope, Alabama. He had joined a general practice group made up of five doctors. The clinic was located in the town of Spanish Fort, which was halfway between Mobile and Fairhope. He lived and worked close enough to take care of his father and far enough away that memories of the past would remain murky instead of vivid.

It had been carnival season when he'd left for LA. He'd been riding high on being the king. His queen had been his girlfriend for the last two years and one of the most beautiful girls in Mobile society. He'd gotten his pick of medical fellowships that had allowed him to only be a few hours away in Birmingham. Gossips had it that he and his queen would ride off into the happily-ever-after as soon as he finished his fellowship. Mark had not planned to disappoint them. That was until he and Mike had decided they needed to drive to the beach after the krewe dance on Fat Tuesday night.

How many times since he'd been back had he picked up the phone to call and see how Mike was doing? How many times had he not followed through? He'd seen Mike a few times over the years. Those had been brief and uncomfortable meetings. Mark had always left with another wheelbarrow of guilt piled on top of the mountain that was already there.

He and Mike had made big plans. They had both been on their way to Birmingham, Mark to complete his fellowship and Mike to earn his Master's in Business. They would return to town to set up a clinic practice, Mark handling the medical end and Mike overseeing the business side. They'd even talked about their families building homes next door to each other. But after the accident Mike's longtime girlfriend had left him. Those dreams vanished. Because of Mark.

As time had gone by it had become easier to satisfy his need to know how Mike was doing by asking others about him. Often when Mark had spoken to his father he'd ask about Mike. His father had always encouraged him to call and talk to Mike if he wanted to know how he was doing. Mark hadn't. That way the guilt didn't become a throbbing, breathing thing.

Mark pushed the front doorbell of his father's house then opened the door. He was met in the high-ceilinged hall by John, the man who had worked for Mark, Sr. since Mark, Jr. had been a boy.

"Hi. How's he doing today?"

"Your dad has had a good day. He's out by the pool."

Mark headed down the all-too-familiar hall that led through the middle of the house and out onto the brick patio with the pool beyond. His father sat in a wheelchair in the sun, with his nurse nearby, reading a book. Mark winced at the sight. It hurt his heart to see the strong, commanding man brought to this by a stroke. Only with time and patience and massive amounts of physical therapy would he regain enough strength to walk again. At least his father had a chance of getting out of the chair, unlike Mike, who had no choice.

Mark circled his father so he faced him. "Hi, Dad."

His white-haired father gave him a lopsided smile. "Hello, son."

Fortunately his mind was still strong. His nurse closed her book and after a nod to Mark made her way toward the house.

Mark pulled a metal pool chair close so he

could sit where his father could see him. "How are you doing today?"

"Fine. Emmett has been by to tell me what went on at the board meeting. He said you didn't make it."

"No, I had patients to see. We've talked about this already. You've put good people in place to handle the company. Let them do it."

"It's not the same. We need a Clayborn there."

"I know, Dad."

His father continued. "I'm glad you stopped by. I wanted to talk to you about attending the krewe dance next week. I can't go and our family needs to be represented. You're the only one to do it."

Mark had always enjoyed the fanfare and glamour of The Mystical Order of Orion dance, the visit from the king and queen and their court. But after what had happened twelve years ago he was hesitant to attend. He took a deep breath. "It's not really my thing anymore but I know it's important to you to keep up appearances."

"You were king. That is and was a high honor. You owe it to the krewe, to the Clayborn name to attend."

"I know, Dad. I'll do my duty."

"This used to be your favorite time of the year. You need to let yourself off the hook, son. It wasn't your fault."

Maybe everyone thought that but Mark sure didn't. He carried the horror of what had happened to Mike with him daily. Now that he was back in Mobile it was more alive than it had ever been. Time hadn't healed the wound, only covered it over.

Mark had dinner with his father then headed across the bay to Fairhope, a small township where the family summer home was located. When he'd arrived in Alabama he'd needed a place to live. Staying in Fairhope gave him a house of his own, a safe haven. Since he was working at a clinic in Spanish Fort, a city just north of Fairhope, living there was convenient.

Entering the large dark room with hardwood paneling, Mark walked through to the family-style kitchen. There he pulled a drink out of the refrigerator and went out to the deck. Mobile Bay stretched far and wide before him. He could see the tall buildings of the city in the distance. The wind had picked up, rustling the shrubbery around the deck. A seagull swooped down and plucked a fish out of the water near the end of the pier. No, this wasn't LA anymore.

Mark had agreed to pitch in and work the parades as a first responder when one of his new partners had said that they did that as a public service during Mardi Gras season. He'd agreed to do his part but had expected that it would be in some of the surrounding smaller towns. When he'd been assigned the parade in downtown Mobile he hadn't felt like he could say no. He needed to be a team player since he'd only joined the medical group a few months earlier. Despite the parade location, Mark had enjoyed the assignment. Especially helping the young girl. Her mother had been attractive. More than once since then he'd wondered where she worked.

He'd spent the rest of the parade scanning the crowd. His chest still contracted at the thought he might see Mike. He'd spent years making a point of not thinking about the automobile accident. Now that he was back it seemed the only thing on his mind.

His cell phone rang. He pulled it out of his pocket. "This is Dr. Clayborn."

"Hey, Mark, it's Ralph. We need you again the

day after tomorrow if you can help us out. Afternoon parade in Dauphine."

He didn't mind working a parade in Dauphine. It was on his side of the bay. As long as it wasn't in Mobile. There the chance of facing his past became greater. "Yeah, I'm only seeing patients in the morning. Will I be on a bike again?"

"Not this time. I just need you at the med tent. It'll be set up in the First Baptist Church parking lot."

"I'll be there."

"Marsha?" Laura Jo called as she and Allie opened the door of her best friend's apartment Wednesday afternoon.

"Hey, we're back here," a voice came from the direction of the kitchen area located in the back of the apartment.

She followed Allie down the short hallway to find Marsha and her son, Jeremy, decorating a wagon with purple, green and gold ribbons.

Marsha looked up as they entered. "You know Mardi Gras almost kills me every year. I say I'm not going to do anything next year then here I am, doing even more."

Allie had already joined in to help Jeremy with the decorations.

"I know what you mean. It makes working in the ER interesting. I've enjoyed my day off but I'll pay for it, no doubt, by being on the night shift. I appreciate you letting Allie spend the night."

"It's not a problem. I love her like my own." She ruffled Allie's hair.

Laura Jo had met Marsha at the Mothers Without Partners clinic. Phil had lived up to all her father's predictions and more when he'd left her pregnant and cleaned out their bank account to never be seen again. Even after all these years he hadn't even checked to see if he had a son or daughter. Marsha's husband had died in a fishing accident. She and Marsha had hit it off right away. Circumstances had brought them together but friendship had seen to it that they still depended on each other.

They'd shared an apartment for a few months and had traded off their time watching the kids while the other had worked or gone to school. They had their own apartments now but in the same complex and Marsha was more like family than the one Laura Jo had left behind.

They had joined forces to help other mothers who didn't have anyone to fall back on. They had convinced the city to sell them an old home so these women would have a place to live and receive help while they were getting their lives in order. The deadline to pay for the house was looming. Finding the funding had become more difficult than Laura Jo had anticipated.

Marsha announced, "I heard from the city contact. He said we had to move soon on the house or the city will have to announce it's for sale. They can't hold it forever."

Laura Jo groaned. That wasn't what she wanted to hear. "How much time do we have?"

"Week or two. At least until things settle down after Mardi Gras. We've got to come up with a good way to raise a lot of money. Fast. I know you don't want to do it but you do have the contacts. Maybe you could put on a party dress and go pick the pockets of all those society friends you used to hang around with."

Laura Jo shook her head. "That's not going to happen. We'll have to find another way."

What if she had to face her mother and father? Worse, have them see her asking for money. That's what they had thought she'd be doing if she married Phil. That's what he'd wanted her to do, but she'd refused. After her fight with her parents she and Phil had gone to Las Vegas that night to get married.

When they'd returned Phil had left to work on an oil rig. Three weeks later he'd come home. A week later all his pay had gone and he'd admitted he'd been fired. He'd made noises about looking for a job but in hindsight she didn't think he'd ever really tried. Things had got worse between them. The issue that finally snapped them had been Laura Jo telling him she was pregnant. Phil's snarling parting words were, "I didn't sign on for no kid. You can't put that on me. Having you is bad enough."

Marsha gave her questioning look. "You know I'm kidding but…"

"I'll come up with something." She checked her watch. "Now, I have to get to the hospital." Stepping toward Allie, Laura Jo said to Marsha, "I'll meet you at the parade tomorrow evening."

"Sounds like a plan."

Laura Jo leaned down and kissed Allie on the head. "See ya. Be good for Marsha."

"I will," Allie replied, then returned to what she was doing.

"Thanks, Marsha." Laura Jo called as she went up the hall.

Six hours later, Laura Jo was longing for her dinner and a moment to put her feet up. She wasn't going to get either anytime soon. Working in a trauma one level hospital meant a constant influx of patients, not only the regular cases but Mardi Gras's as well, which brought out the revelers and daredevils. Weekend nights were the worst and the place resembled a circus with not enough clowns to go around. Everyone had their hands full. The doors were swishing open regularly with people coming in. The constant ringing of the phone filled the area, blending with the piercing scream of ambulance sirens.

As she stepped back into the nursing station the phone rang again. Seconds later the clerk called out, "Incoming. Sixty-seven-year-old male. Heart attack. Resuscitating in transit. Child with head trauma behind that. ETA ten."

"I'll take the heart. Trauma six." Laura Jo hurried to set up what was needed before the patient arrived.

Minutes later the high-pitched sound of the ambulance arriving filled the air and Laura Jo rushed outside. The double rear doors of the vehicle stood wide open. Usually by this time the EMTs would be unloading the patient.

Looking inside, she immediately recognized the EMT working over the patient but not the other man. Then she did. *Mark Clayborn.* Again he was wearing red biking shorts and a yellow shirt of a first responder.

Mark held the portable oxygen bubble away from the patient as the EMT placed the defibrillator paddles on the patient's chest. The body jerked. The beep of the machine monitoring the heart rate started and grew steadier. Putting the earpieces of the stethoscope that had been around his neck into place, Mark listened to the man's heart. "Let's get him inside," he said with a sharp tone of authority. He then made an agile jump to the ground, turned toward the interior of the ambulance and helped bring out the patient on the stretcher.

Although confused by why he had been allowed in the emergency vehicle, she still followed his lead. It was against policy to ride in the back unless you were part of the EMT staff. But now wasn't the time for questions. She stood aside while the two men lifted out the stretcher. The wheels dropped to the pavement and Laura Jo wrapped her hand around the yellow metal frame and pulled. Mark kept his fingers on the pulse point of the patient's wrist while the EMT pushed.

They had reached the doors when Mark said, "We're losing him again."

Tall enough to lean over and push on the patient's chest, he began compressions. Another nurse met them and gave oxygen. Laura Jo kept moving ahead, her arm burning. To her relief, they got the patient into the trauma room. There Mark and the EMT used the defibrillator once again. Seconds later the monitor made a beep and the line went from straight to having peaks and valleys. After they gained a steady pulse, she worked to place leads to the monitors on the patient. The ER doctor rushed in.

Mark and the EMT backed away with exhausted sighs, giving the ER doctor, Laura Jo and the other staff members space to work. For the next twenty intensive minutes, Laura Jo followed the ER doctor's instructions to the letter. Finally they managed to stabilize the patient enough to send him to surgery.

Laura Jo had to talk to the family. They must be scared. When she asked the admission clerk where they were she was told exam room five.

"Why are they in an exam room?"

"The man's granddaughter is being evaluated."

Laura Jo headed for the exam room. It shouldn't have surprised her that Mark was there, too. He came out as she was preparing to go in.

"Well, fancy meeting you here," he drawled in a deep voice that made her think of a dark velvet night.

"It's not that amazing really. I work here."

"I figured that out. So how's your daughter? Healing nicely?"

"She's fine. A little tender but fine."

"Good. By the way, I'm Dr. Mark Clayborn."

"Yes, I know who you are. As in the Clayborn Building, Clayborn Bank, Clayborn Shipping.

He gave her a studying look. "Do I know you?"

"I'm Laura Jo Akins. Used to be Laura Jo Herron."

"Herron? My parents used to talk about the Herrons. Robert Herron. Real estate."

She looked away. "Yes, that's my father."

He had pursed his lips. "Well, that's a surprise. Isn't it a small world?"

Too small for Laura Jo's comfort. It was time to change the subject. "Thanks for helping out. Now I need to talk to the family." She gave the door to the exam room a quick knock and pushed it open.

It turned out that she was wasting her time. "The nice Dr. Clayborn" had updated them and also seen to Lucy, their little girl, but they appreciated Laura Jo coming in. By the time she'd returned to the nursing station things seemed to be under control in the ER. All the exam and trauma rooms were full. The critical cases were being cared for. Those waiting were not serious.

"Why don't you take your supper break while you can?" the lead nurse said.

"Are you sure?"

"It's now or never. You know the closer we get to Fat Tuesday the merrier it gets around here."

Laura Jo laughed. "If merry is what you want to call it. Okay, I'll go."

"I'd rather call it merry otherwise I think I might cry," the lead nurse said with a grin.

Laura Jo grabbed her lunch box. It had become a habit to pack a lunch when money had been so tight even before Phil had left. Reaching the cafeteria, she scanned the room for an empty table. The busy ER translated to a full room. As soon as a table opened up she headed for it. Before she could get to it Mark slid into one of the two seats available. Disappointed, she stopped and looked around for another spot.

He waved her toward him. "You can join me, if you like."

Laura Jo looked at him. Did she really have a choice? She was expected back in the ER soon. "Thank you."

He grinned at her. "You don't sound too excited about it."

What was he expecting her to say? *You're right, I'm not?* "I have to eat. The ER won't stay calm for long."

"It did look a little wild in there. I've certainly had more than my share this evening. I haven't done this much emergency work since I was on my med school rotation. Don't see many head trauma and heart attacks in family practice."

Laura Jo pulled her sandwich out of the plastic bag. "I understand that the girl was sitting on top of her father's shoulders and toppled off. When the grandfather saw what had happened he had a heart attack."

"Yeah. Thank goodness it all happened within running distance of the med tent. For a few minutes there wasn't enough of us medical personal around to handle all that was going on. I'm just glad the girl has regained consciousness and the grandfather is stable."

"The girl will be here for observation for at least one night and the grandfather for much longer, I'm afraid."

He took a large bite of his hamburger and they ate in silence for a while before he asked, "So you knew who I was the other day. Why didn't you say something?"

"There just didn't seem a right moment."

"So you've seen a lot of Mardi Gras."

She straightened her back and looked directly at him. "I'm not that old."

He grinned. "I'm sorry, I didn't mean to imply that."

Laura Jo had to admit he had a nice smile. She grinned. "That's not what it sounded like to me."

"I was just trying to make pleasant conversation and didn't mean—"

"I know you didn't." Still, it would have been nice if he'd at least thought she looked familiar. She'd been invisible to her parents, unimportant to her husband and just this once it would have been nice to have been memorable. But, then, it had been a long time ago.

"So do you attend any of the krewe festivities?" He chewed slowly, as if waiting patiently for her answer.

"No. I don't travel in that social circle anymore." She took a bite of her sandwich.

"Why not? As I remember, the Herrons were a member of the same krewe as my family."

"I'm an Akins now."

"So Mr. Akins isn't a member either, I gather."

"No, and Mr. Akins, as you put it, isn't around to be a member."

"I'm sorry."

"I'm not. He left years ago."

"Oh, I thought…"

"I know. For all I know, he's alive and well somewhere."

Having finished his meal, Mark leaned back in his chair and crossed his arms over his chest. "Well, it has been a pleasure running into you, Ms. Atkins."

Laura Jo stood to leave. "You, too, Dr. Clayborn. We do seem to keep running into each other."

"Why, Ms. Akins, you don't believe in serendipity?"

"If I ever did believe in serendipity, that would've been a long time ago. Now, if you'll excuse me, I need to get back to work."

CHAPTER TWO

ON SATURDAY AFTERNOON Mark made his way through the side streets of Mobile, working around the parade route, which was already blocked off. It was one more week before Mardi Gras weekend and there would be a large parade that afternoon and another that night in downtown Mobile.

Throughout the week in the surrounding towns parades were planned, culminating in three or four per day until the final one on Fat Tuesday. Then Ash Wednesday would arrive and end all the revelry.

He'd been assigned to work in the med tent set up just off Government Street at a fire station. He'd wanted to say no, had even suggested that he work one or two of the parades in a nearby town, but he'd been told that he was needed there. His gut clenched each time he crossed the bay but his partners wouldn't like him not being a team player during this time of the year. Plus, Mark had no desire to admit why going into Mobile bothered him.

All he hoped for now was a slow day, but he didn't expect it. He wanted less drama than the last time he'd worked a med tent a few days earlier. Still, there had been some interesting points.

Dinner with Laura Jo Akins had been the highlight. He had at least found out she wasn't married. And she seemed to be anti-krewe for some reason. He had no doubt that she'd grown up on the social club festivities of a krewe, just like him. Why would she have such a negative view now? Or was her pessimistic attitude directed toward him? Did she know about the accident? His part in it?

Laura Jo Akins also appeared to be one of those women who knew her mind and stood her ground, but it also seemed there was a venerable spot to her, too. As if she hid something from the world. What was that all about?

Mark looked over the crowd again. At least she took his thoughts off worrying that he might see Mike at a parade. He looked forward to seeing her pixie face if they ever met again. People were creatures of habit and usually showed up in the same places to watch the parades. He wasn't sure why she interested him so, but she'd popped into his head a number of times over the past few days.

He had been at the med tent long enough to introduce himself to some of the other volunteers when he looked up to see none other than Laura Jo walking toward the tent. She caught sight of him about the same time. He didn't miss her moment of hesitation before she continued in his direction. He smiled and nodded at her. She returned his smile.

A few minutes later he was asked to help with a woman who was having an asthma attack in the unseasonably warm weather. It was some time later before he had a chance to speak to Laura Jo.

"I believe we might be caught in some Mardi Gras mystical mojo," he said, low enough that the others around them couldn't hear.

"I don't believe any sort of thing. I'm more of the dumb luck kind of person," she responded, as she continued to sort supplies.

He chuckled. "Didn't expect to see me again so soon, did you?"

She spun around, her hands going to her hips. "Did you plan this?"

"I did not," he said with complete innocence. "I was told when and where to be."

"I thought maybe with the Clayborn name..."

What did she have against the Clayborns? Did she know what he'd done? If she did, he couldn't blame her for not wanting to have anything to do with him. "Excuse me?"

"Nothing."

"Dr. Clayborn, we need you," one of the other volunteers called.

Mark had no choice but to go to work.

Half an hour later, the sound of a jazz band rolled down the street. Because the med tent was set up at the fire station, no one could park or stand in front of it. Mark and the others had an unobstructed view of the parade. Thankfully there was no one requiring help so they all stepped out toward the street curb to watch. Laura Jo seemed to appreciate the parade. She even swayed to the music of "Let the good times roll."

He wandered over to stand just behind her. "You enjoy a good parade as much as your daughter does, I see." Mark couldn't help but needle her. She reacted so prettily to it.

"Yes, I love a good parade. You make it sound like it should be a crime."

"And you make it sound like it's a crime that I noticed," he shot back.

"No crime. Just not used to someone taking that much notice."

"That's hard to believe. You mean there's no man who pays attention to you?"

"Getting a little personal, aren't you, Doctor?" She glanced back at him.

"No, just making conversation."

"Hey, Mom."

They both turned at the sound of Laura Jo's daughter's voice. She was with another woman about Laura Jo's age and there was a boy with them about the same height as the daughter.

Before her mother could respond the girl said to Mark, "I know you. You're that man who helped me the other day. Look, my hands are all better." She put out her hands palms up. "My knee still hurts a little." She lifted her denim-covered knee.

"And I know you." He smiled down at her. "But forgive me, I've forgotten your name."

"Allie."

He squatted down to her level. "I'm glad you're feeling better, Allie." Standing again, he glanced in the direction of the woman he didn't know. Laura Jo must have gotten the hint because she said, "This is Marsha Gilstrap. A friend of mine." She looked toward the boy. "And Jeremy, her son. I thought ya'll were going to watch the parade over on Washington."

"We wanted to come by and say hi to you," Allie said.

Laura Jo gave her daughter a hug then looked down at her with what Mark recognized as unbounded love. He liked it when he saw parents who really cared about their children. Her actions hadn't just been for show when her daughter had been hurt at the parade. She truly cared about her child. He recognized that love because his parents had had the same for him. That's why his father had insisted Mark not get involved with Mike's case after the accident. His father had feared what it might do to Mark's future. He been young enough and scared enough that he'd agreed, despite the guilt he'd felt over leaving the way he had. Now he didn't trust himself to get close enough to care about someone. If he did, he might fail them, just as he had Mike. He hadn't stood beside Mike, whom he'd loved like a brother, so why would he have what it took to stand by a wife and family?

A float coming by drew Allie's attention. Mark put a hand on her shoulder. "Come on. This is a great spot to watch a parade."

Allie looked at her mother in question. Laura Jo took a second before she gave an agreeable nod but he got the sense that she didn't want to.

Allie glanced at the boy. "Can Jeremy come, too?"

"Sure."

Jeremy's mother, in contrast to Laura Jo, was all smiles about the boy joining them.

"We'll just be right up here if you need us." Mark made an effort to give Laura Jo his most charming smile.

He nudged one of the volunteers out of the way so that the children had a front-row place to stand. A couple of times he had to remind them not to step out beyond the curve. Because they were standing in front of the fire station, there were no barriers in place. After a few minutes Laura Jo and her friend joined them.

"Thanks, we'll take these two off your hands," Laura Jo said, as if she was helping him out. What she was really doing was trying to get rid of him.

"Look at the dog. How funny." Allie squealed. The dog was wearing a vest and a hat. "I wish I had a dog to dress up. Then we could be in a parade."

Laura Jo placed her hand on top of Allie's shoulder. "Maybe one day, honey."

There was something in the wispy tone in the girl's voice that got to him. It reminded him of how he'd sounded the first time he'd asked if he could be in a dog parade. When he and his brother had participated in a parade it had been one of the greatest pleasures of his childhood. He could surely give that to Allie without becoming too involved in her and her mother's lives. "You could borrow my dog. Gus would be glad to let you dress him up," Mark offered.

"Could I, Mom?" Allie looked at Laura Jo as if her life depended on a positive answer.

"I don't know."

"I think Allie and Gus would make a great pair." He had no doubt Laura Jo hated to say no to something her daughter so obviously wanted to do. But why was he making it his job to see that Allie had a chance to be in a parade? Was it because Laura Jo was a hard-working mother who couldn't do this for her daughter and it was easy enough for him to do? It would be a great memory for Allie, just as it had been for him.

"Please, Mom."

"Fairhope has a parade on Sunday evening that I believe dogs are allowed in. Why don't you and Allie come and meet Gus that afternoon? You could bring some clothes for him and see how he likes them."

Laura Jo gave him a piercing look that said she wasn't pleased with the turn of events.

In a perverse way he liked the idea he was able to nettle her.

"Allie, I don't think we should take advantage of Dr. Clayborn's time."

"Please, call me Mark. And I don't mind." He really didn't. Since he'd been back in town he had kept to himself. It would be nice to spend the afternoon with someone. "I'm sure Gus will be glad to have the company. I've not been around much the past few days. Marsha, you and Jeremy are welcome, too."

"Thanks. It sounds like fun but I can't. Jeremy can if Laura Jo doesn't mind," Marsha said, smiling.

Laura Jo shot Marsha a look as if there would be more to say about this when they were alone.

"Mom, please," Allie pleaded. "Please."

"Won't your wife mind us barging in? Won't your children be dressing him up?"

"No wife. No children. So there's no reason you can't."

"Then I guess we could come by for a little while but I'm not making any promises about the parade." Laura Jo looked down at Allie.

"Great. I'll expect you about two. Here's my address." He pulled out a calling card, turned it over and, removing a pen from his pocket, wrote on it. "I'll have Gus all bathed and waiting on you."

Allie giggled. "Okay."

Mark looked at Laura Jo. "See you tomorrow."

She gave him a weak smile and he grinned. He was already looking forward to the afternoon.

* * *

Laura Jo wasn't sure how she'd managed to be coerced into agreeing to go to Mark's. Maybe it was because of the look of anticipation on Allie's face or the maternal guilt she felt whenever Allie asked to do something and she had to say no because she had to go to work or school. Now that she was in a position to give her child some fun in her life, she couldn't bring herself to say no. But going to Mark Clayborn's house had to be one for the record. She didn't really know the man. She'd admired him with a young girl's hero worship. But she knew little about the man he had become. He'd been nice enough so far but she hadn't always been the best judge of character.

She'd searched for a sound reason why they couldn't do it. Marsha certainly hadn't been any help. It was as if she had pushed her into going. For once Laura Jo wished she had to work on Sunday. But no such luck.

Allie was up earlier than usual in her excitement over the possibility of being in the dog parade. Jeremy had been almost as bad, Marsha said, when he ran to meet them at the car later that day.

"So are you looking forward to an afternoon with the handsome, debonair and rich Dr. Mark Clayborn?" Marsha asked with a grin.

They'd had a lively and heated discussion over a cup of coffee late the night before about Mark. Marsha seemed to think she should develop him as an ally in funding the single mothers' house. Laura Jo wasn't so sure. That was a road she'd promised herself she'd never go down again. She wasn't ever going to ask her parents or her society friends for anything ever again. That certainly included Mark Clayborn.

After today she didn't plan to see him again. This afternoon was about Allie and seeing a smile on her face. That only. Allie had been begging for a dog for the past year but they didn't have a lifestyle that was good for taking care of a dog.

Laura Jo pulled her aging compact car off the winding, tree-shaded road into the well-groomed, riverbed-pebbled drive of the address she'd been given. The crunch made a familiar sound. Her own family's place just a few miles down the road had the same type of drive, or at least it had the last time she'd been there.

The foliage of the large trees with moss hanging from them gave the area a cozy feel. Soon she entered an open space where a sweeping, single-story beach house sat with a wide expanse of yard between it and the bay beyond.

"Do you see Gus?" Allie strained at her seat belt as she peered out the window.

"Now, honey, I don't want you to get your hopes up too high. Gus may not like being dressed up." Laura Jo didn't want to say "or you." Some owners thought their dogs loved everyone when they often didn't.

"He'll like it, I know he will."

"I think he will, too," Jeremy said from the backseat.

Laura Jo looked at him in the rearview mirror and smiled. "We'll see."

She pulled to a stop behind a navy blue high-end European car. To Mark's credit, it wasn't a sports car but it was finer than Laura Jo had ever ridden in, even when she'd still been living with her parents.

Her door had hardly opened before Allie ran toward a basset hound, whose ears dragged along the ground. Not far behind him strolled Mark. For a second her breath caught. He had all the markers of an eye-catching man. Tall, blond wavy hair and an air about him that said he could take care of himself and anyone else he cared about. It was a dazzling combination.

She'd been asked out a number of times by one of the men at the hospital, but she'd never had a man both irritate her and draw her to him at the same time. That was exactly what Mark Clayborn did.

He looked down with a smile at Allie, with her arms wrapped around Gus, and Jeremy, patting him, then at Laura Jo.

Her middle fluttered. If it wasn't for all the baggage she carried, her inability to trust her judgment of men, maybe she might be interested. She'd let Allie have her day and make a concerted effort not to see Mark again.

"Hey. Did you have any trouble finding it?"

"No trouble. I knew which one it was when you told me you lived in Fairhope."

"Really?"

"I remember passing it when I was a kid." She'd been aware all her life where the Clayborn summer home was located.

He glanced back to where the children played with the dog. "I think they're hitting it off."

Laura Jo couldn't help but agree.

"Allie, did you bring some clothes for Gus? I got a few things just in case you didn't," Mark said, strolling toward the kids and dog.

"They're in the car."

"I'll get them, honey," Laura Jo called, as the kids headed toward the large open yard between the house and bay. "Don't go near the water and stay where I can see you."

She walked to the car and Mark followed her. "You're a good mother."

Laura Jo glanced at him. "I try to be."

"So when did Allie's father leave?"

Laura Jo opened the passenger door then looked at him. "When I was three months pregnant."

Mark whistled. "That explains some of your standoffishness."

She pulled a large brown sack out of the car and closed the door with more force than necessary. "I'm not."

"Yeah, you are. For some reason, you don't want to like me, even when you do."

She was afraid he might be right. Thankfully,

squealing in the front yard drew their attention to the two children running around as a dog almost as wide as he was tall chased them.

Mark checked his watch and called, "Allie and Jeremy, we need to get started on what Gus will wear because the parade starts in a couple of hours."

The kids ran toward them and Gus followed.

"Why don't we go around to the deck where it's cooler? We can dress Gus there," Mark said to the kids.

Mark led the way with the kids and Gus circled them. Laura Jo hung back behind them. Mark was good with children. Why didn't he have a wife and kids of his own? She imagined she was the only one of many who didn't fall at his charming feet.

The deck was amazing. It was open at one end. Chairs and a lounge group were arranged into comfortable conversation areas. At the other end was an arbor with a brown vine that must be wisteria on it. Laura Jo could only envision what it would look like in the spring and summer, with its green leaves creating a roof of protection from the sun. She'd love to sit in a comfortable chair under it but that wasn't going to happen.

"Allie, why don't you and Jeremy pull the things you brought out of the bag while I go get what I bought? Then you can decide how to dress Gus."

Allie took the bag from Laura Jo. With the children busy pulling feather boas, old hair bows, purple, green and gold ribbon from the bag, Laura Jo took a seat on the end of a lounge chair and watched.

Mark quickly returned with an armload of stuff.

"I thought you only got a few things," Laura Jo said.

He grinned. Her heart skipped a beat.

"I might have gotten a little carried away." He looked directly at her. "I do that occasionally."

For some reason, she had the impression he might be talking about sex. She hadn't had a thought like that in forever. Not since Phil had left. He'd made it clear that she hadn't been wanted and neither had their child.

Mark added his armload to the growing pile on the deck.

"Okay, Allie, I want you and Jeremy to pick out a winning combination. They give prizes for the funniest dog, best dressed, most spirited and some more I don't remember. Let's try to win a prize," Mark said, as he joined them on the planks of the wooden deck and held Gus. "I'll hold him while you dress him."

Laura Jo scooted back in the lounge to watch. It was a February day but the sun was shining. It wasn't long until her eyes closed.

She didn't know how long she'd been out before Mark's voice above her said, "You'd better be careful or you'll get burned. Even the winter sun in the south can get you."

"Thanks. I'm well aware of that. Remember, I've lived here all my life."

"That's right, a Herron."

"Who is a Herron, Mommy?"

"They're a family I used to know."

Mark's brows rose.

"Now, let me see what ya'll have done to Gus while I was napping," Laura Jo said quickly, before he could ask any more questions in front of Allie.

Mark didn't question further, seeing that Laura Jo didn't want to talk about her family in front of

Allie. But he would be asking later. Allie didn't even know who her grandparents were? There was a deep, dark secret there that he was very interested in finding out about. Why hadn't he recognized Laura Jo? Probably because she had been too young to take his notice. His mouth drew into a line. More likely, he had been so focused on his world he hadn't looked outside it.

"My, doesn't Gus look, uh...festive?"

Mark couldn't help but grin at Laura Jo's description. Festive was a good word for it, along with silly. His dog wore a purple, gold and green feather boa wrapped around his neck. A dog vest of the same colors was on his body, bands on his ankles and a bow on the end of his tail. This being the one thing Allie had insisted he needed. Mark was amazed the Gus was as agreeable as he was about that.

Allie pronounced him "Perfect."

"I think we should be going if we want to make the start time."

"Start time?" Laura Jo asked.

"For the Mystic Mutts parade."

"I don't think—"

"We can't miss it. Isn't that right, Allie and Jeremy?"

"Right," both children said in unison.

Great. Now she was being ganged up on.

"Come on, Mommy. We have to take Gus," Allie pleaded.

Laura Jo glared at Mark. "I guess I don't have much of a choice."

Allie and Jeremy danced around her. "Yay."

"Let me get Gus's leash and we'll be all set." Mark went inside and returned with a lead.

As they rounded the house and headed toward the cars he looked at Laura Jo's. It was too small for all of them.

"I don't think we can all get in my car," Laura Jo said from beside him.

Mark stopped and looked at hers again. "I guess I should drive."

"You don't sound like you really want to do that. We could take two cars but I'm sure parking will be tight."

Mark's lips drew into a tight line. The thought of being responsible for Laura Jo and the kids gave him a sick feeling. Children had never ridden in his car. Since the accident he'd made it a practice not to drive with others in the car if he could help it. Often he hired a driver when he went out on a date. Unable to come up with another plan, he said, "Then we'll go in my car. Please make sure the children are securely buckled in."

Laura Jo gave him an odd look before she secured Allie and Jeremy in the backseat. Gus found a spot between them and Allie placed an arm around him. Laura Jo joined him in the front. Mark looked back to check if the children were buckled in.

"Is there a problem?" Laura Jo asked.

If he kept this up he would make them all think he was crazy. He eased his grip on the steering wheel and let the blood flow back into his knuckles. "No. I was just double-checking they were okay."

Laura Jo shook her head as she ran a hand across the leather of the seat. "Worried about having kids in your fancy car?"

"No."

"Nice," she murmured.

"Like my car?"

"Yes," she said, more primly than the situation warranted, as she placed her hand in her lap.

He grinned. At least this subject took his mind off having a carload of passengers. "It's okay to say what you think."

"I wouldn't think it's very practical. The cost of a car like this could help a lot of people in need."

"I help people in need all the time. I also give to charities so I don't feel guilty about owning this car." Taking a fortify breath, he started it and pulled away from the house. At the end of the drive, he turned onto the road leading into town.

"I'm just not impressed by fancy cars and houses. People with those think they can tell you what to do, how you need to live. Even look down on others."

He glanced at her. "That's an interesting statement. Care to give me some background?"

"No, not really."

"Well, you just insulted me and my family and yours as well, and you won't even do me the courtesy of telling me why?"

"I'm sorry I insulted you. Sometimes my mouth gets ahead of my brain." She looked out the side window.

Yes, he was definitely going to find out what gave her such a sour view of people with money. He'd always prided himself on the amount he gave to charities. He had nothing to be ashamed of where that was concerned. Standing beside someone he loved when there was a disaster was where he failed.

A few minutes later he pulled the car into a tight space a couple of blocks from the parade route. It was the only spot he could find after circling the area. How had he gotten through the short drive without breaking into a sweat? Amazingly, talking to Laura Jo had made him forget his anxiety over driving. "This is the best I can do. We'll have to walk some."

Laura Jo saw to getting the children out. He leashed Gus and then gave him over to Allie. The girl beamed.

"I checked the paper this morning and the start of the parade is at the corner of Section and Third Street."

They weaved their way through the already growing crowd. As the number of people increased, Mark took Gus's leash from Allie and made sure that space was made for the dog, children and Laura Jo. A few times he touched her waist to direct her through a gap in the crowd. At the first occurrence she stiffened and glanced back at him. When he did it again she seemed to take it in her stride.

Mark was pleased when his little party arrived at the starting line without a loss of personnel. He looked at Laura Jo. "Why don't you wait here with the kids while I check in?"

"We'll be right over here near the brick wall." She took Gus's lead and led Allie and Jeremy to the spot she'd indicated.

"I'll be right back."

"You hope." She smiled.

It was the first genuine one he'd seen her give. It caught him off guard. It took him a second to respond. "Yeah."

Fifteen minutes later he had Gus, Allie and Jeremy signed in for the parade. He found Laura Jo and the kids waiting right where she'd said they would be. She had her head down, listening to something that Jeremy was saying. The angle of her head indicated she was keeping an eye on her daughter at the same time. Once again he was impressed by her mothering skills. The women he'd gone out with had never shown any interest in being mothers. He'd always thought he'd like to be a father, but he wouldn't let that happen. What if he ran out on them, like he had Mike, when the going got tough? He couldn't take that chance.

There was nothing flashy or pretentious about Laura Jo. More like what you saw was what you got. He'd grown up within the finely drawn lines of what was expected by the tight-knit Mobile society. He hadn't met many women who'd seemed to live life on their own terms. Even in California the women he'd dated had always worn a false front, literally and physically.

Laura Jo's face was devoid of makeup and she wore a simple blouse and jeans with flats. She reminded him of a girl just out of high school. That was until she opened her mouth, then she left no doubt she was a grown woman who could defend herself and her child. Nothing about her indicated she had been raised in one of local society's finest families.

Allie said something and Laura Jo turned her head. Both mother and child had similar coloring. Pretty in an early-spring-leaves-unfolding sort of way. Easy on the eye. Why would any man leave the two of them?

If he ever had a chance to have something as good in his life as they were, he'd hold on to them and never let them out of his sight. He sighed. What he saw between Laura Jo and Allie wasn't meant for him. It wasn't his to have. He'd taken that chance from Mike and he had no right to have it himself. What they had he couldn't be trusted with.

"Hey, there's Dr. Clayborn," Allie called.

Mark grinned as he joined them. He ruffled Allie's hair. "That's Mark to you. Dr. Clayborn sounds like a mouthful for such a little girl."

Allie drew herself up straight. "I'm a big girl."

Mark went down on one knee, bringing himself to eye level with Allie. "I apologize. Yes, you are a big girl. Big enough to walk with Gus in the parade?"

"Really, you're going to let me take Gus in the parade?"

"Yes, and Jeremy, too. But I have to come along with you."

She turned to Laura Jo. "Mommy, I'm going to get to be in the parade."

"I heard, honey, but I don't know."

"I'll be right there with them the entire time." Mark reassured Laura Jo.

The look of hesitation on her face gave him the idea that she didn't often trust Allie's care to anyone but her friend Marsha.

He reached for Gus's leash and she handed it to him. The nylon was warm from her clasp. "She'll be perfectly safe. We'll meet you and Jeremy at the car when it's over. The parade route isn't long."

"I guess it'll be okay." She looked at Allie. "You and Jeremy do just what Mark tells you to do." Laura Jo pinned Mark with a look. "And you turn up with my daughter and Jeremy at the end of the parade."

"Yes, ma'am." He gave her a smile and a little salute. "I'll take good care of them, I promise. Let's go, kids. We need to get in line."

Laura Jo watched as Mark took her daughter's much smaller hand in his larger one and Jeremy's in his other one. Gus walked at Allie's heels as they were swallowed up by the crowd.

What was it about Mark that made her trust him with the most precious person in her life?

She'd never allowed anyone but Marsha that privilege. Maybe it was the way he'd care for Allie's knee, or his devotion to the grandfather and later the girl he'd cared for. Somehow Mark had convinced her in a few short meetings that he could be trusted. Now that she was a mother she better understood how her parents had felt when she had insisted on going off with someone they hadn't trusted.

Alone, she made her way through the crowd to the curb of a street about halfway along the parade route. Taking a seat on the curb, she waited until the parade approached. For this parade there would be no bands involved. All the music would come from music boxes pulled in carts by children. The floats would be decorated wagons and dogs of all shapes and sizes.

Twenty minutes later the first of the parade members came into view. Not far behind them were Allie, Jeremy and Mark. Laura Jo stood as they approached. She'd never seen a larger smile on Allie's face. Mark and Jeremy were grinning also. Gus was lumbering behind them, looking bored but festive. Allie held his leash proudly.

She screamed and waved as they came by.

Allie and Jeremy waved enthusiastically back at her. Mark acknowledged her also. As they came closer he stepped over to Laura Jo and said, "The kids are having a blast."

Laura Jo smiled.

An hour later Laura Jo stood waiting outside Mark's car. Anxiousness was building with every minute that passed. Something had to have gone wrong. Mark and the children should have been there by now. Had something happened to one of the kids? She shouldn't have let them out of her sight. Was this how her parents had felt when she'd run off with Phil?

He had been a master of manipulation. Before they'd got married he'd made her believe he had a good job and he would take care of her. "Don't worry about what your parents think, I'll take care of you," he would say. The worst thing was that he'd made her believe he'd loved her.

Had she let Mark do the same thing? Persuade her to let the kids be in the parade. Had she made a poor character judgment call again? This time with her daughter? Her palms dampened. She'd promised herself to be careful. Now look what was happening. She headed in the direction of where the parade had ended, and soon recognized Mark's tall figure coming in her way. He pulled a wagon on which Gus, Allie and Jeremy rode. With relief filling her chest, she ran toward them.

Mark was red-faced. Jeremy wore a smile. Allie looked pleased with herself as she held Gus's head in her lap. The dog was wearing a crown.

"Where have ya'll been? I was getting worried." Laura Jo stopped beside them.

"Mommy, we won first place for the slowest dog in the parade." Allie beamed.

Laura Jo gave her a hug. "That's wonderful, honey."

"Sorry we made you worry. I should have given you my cell number. Gus also got slower after the parade. I carried him halfway here until I saw a kid with a wagon. I had to give him fifty dollars for it so I could haul Gus back."

At the sound of disgust in Mark's voice Laura Jo couldn't help but laugh. His look of complete exasperation and her sense of relief made the situation even more humorous.

"I'm glad someone thinks it's funny." Mark chuckled.

Laura Jo had to admit he was a good sport and he'd certainly made her daughter happy. Every time she tried to stop laughing she'd think of Mark begging a boy for his wagon and she'd burst out in laughter again. It had been a long time since she'd laughed hard enough to bring tears to her eyes.

"If you think you can stop laughing at me for a few minutes, we can load up this freeloader…" he gave the dog a revolted look "…and get him home."

"Had a workout, did you?" Laura Jo asked, trying to suppress the giggles that kept bubbling up.

"Yeah. No good deed goes unpunished."

"Whose idea was it to be in the parade?"

"Okay, it was mine."

Laura Jo burst into another round of snickers.

"Mommy, are you all right?" Allie looked at her in wonder.

"Oh, honey. I'm fine. I'm just glad you had a good time." She looked over the top of her head and grinned at Mark. Had it really been that long since Allie had seen her laugh?

Mark scooped Gus up in his arms. "If you'll get the door, I'll get this prima donna in the car."

Laura Jo's snort escaped as she opened the door. Allie climbed in next to the dog then Jeremy clambered in. Laura Jo saw they were buckled in. Mark put the wagon in the trunk and slapped the lid down harder than necessary.

"So you plan on being in another parade anytime soon?" she asked him, as she took her place in the front seat.

Mark sneered at her as he started the car. Laura Jo's smile grew. Before they left the parking spot, he twisted to study the children. As he turned the first corner, she looked back to find both of the children asleep. Most of the people at their end of the parade had left already, which made it easy for him to maneuver out of town and back to his home.

As they drove down the drive, Laura Jo said, "Thanks for going to so much trouble for Allie. She had the time of her life."

"You're welcome. Despite Gus being in slow motion, I enjoyed it. I've been a part of a number of parades in my time but never one like today's."

Laura Jo grinned. Something she seemed to

have been doing more of lately. "Well, I appreciate it. I'll get the kids loaded up and we'll get out of your hair."

"Mommy, I'm hungry."

Laura Jo sighed and looked back at her daughter. "I thought you were asleep."

"I bet they are hungry. They've had a busy day. I've got some hot dogs I could put on the grill," Mark suggested, as he pulled the car to a stop.

"You've already done enough. I think we had better go." Laura Jo didn't want to like him any more than she already did, and she was afraid she might if she stayed around Mark much longer. The picture of him pulling the dog and Allie and Jeremy put a warm spot in her heart. He wasn't the self-centered man she'd believed he might be.

"Can't I play with Gus a little while longer?" Allie pleaded.

"Face it, you're not going to win this one." Mark grinned.

"You're sure about this?" Laura Jo realized she'd lost again.

"Yeah. It'll be nice to have company for a meal."

"Okay," she said to Mark, then turned and

looked at Allie. "We'll stay for a little while longer but when I say it's time to go, we go without any argument, understood?"

"Yes, ma'am," Allie said, and Jeremy, who had awoken, nodded in agreement.

Laura Jo opened the door for Allie while Mark did the same for Jeremy and Gus.

"If you both give your mom and me just a few minutes, we'll have the hot dogs ready. Why don't you guys watch the parade on TV? Look for us."

"Do you think they'll have it running already?" Laura Jo asked.

"They should. When I told friends on the West Coast that we had Mardi Gras parades on TV they were amazed." Mark turned to the kids again. "I'll turn the TV on and we'll give it a look."

They all followed Mark through the front door of the house. Laura Jo studied the interior. The foyer had an easy, casual feel to it but every piece of furniture was placed so that it reminded her of a home decorating magazine. From the entrance, it opened into a large space with an exterior glass wall that gave the room a one-hundred-and-eighty-degree view of the deck area and the bay. Full ceiling-to-floor green-checked curtains were pushed back to either side of the windowed area. The late-afternoon sunlight streamed into the room, giving it an inviting glow.

Overstuffed cream-colored couches faced each other. A table with a chess set on it sat to one side of the room. Opposite it there was a large-screen TV built into the wall, with bookshelves surrounding it. Comfortable-looking armchairs were placed throughout the room. The house gave her the feeling that a family had lived and loved here.

"What a wonderful room," Laura Jo whispered.

"Thanks. It's my favorite space."

She turned, startled, to find Mark standing close. She had been so caught up in the room she hadn't noticed him approach.

"I'll turn the TV on for the kids then get started on those dogs. You don't need to help. You're welcome to stay with them."

"No, I said I would help and I will. After all, I haven't carried a dog around town all afternoon," she said with a grin.

"You're not going to let that go, are you?" He gave her a pained look.

She shook her head. "The visual is just too good to let go of."

He picked up a remote and pushed a button. The TV came on. The kids had already found themselves a place on a sofa. After a few changes of channels he stopped. "I do believe this is ours."

"You guys stay right here. Don't go outside," Laura Jo said.

Mark headed toward the open kitchen Laura Jo could see off to the left. She followed. It was a modern and up-to-date space that was almost as large as her entire apartment. She ran a hand across the granite of the large counter in the middle of the room with a sigh of pleasure. "I wish I had a place like this to cook. I bet you could make a perfect king cake on this top," she murmured, more to herself than Mark.

"You're welcome to come over anytime and use it. I get nowhere near the use out of it that I should." Mark put his head in the refrigerator and came out with a package of hot dogs.

"Thanks for the offer. But I don't really have time to do a lot of cooking." She wished she did have. Even if she did, she wouldn't be coming here to do it.

"That's not what Allie led me to believe." He picked through a drawer and found some tongs.

"I'd like to but I don't think we'll be getting that friendly."

He came to stand across the counter from her. "Why not? You might find you like me if you'd give me a chance."

"We're from two different worlds now and I don't see us going any further than we did today."

"What do you mean by two different worlds? Our parents have been acquaintances for years. I don't see that we are that different."

Had she hurt his feelings? No, she couldn't imagine that what she thought or felt mattered that much to him. But he had been nice to Allie and he deserved the truth. "I have nothing to do with that society stuff anymore."

"I had no idea you were such a snob, or is it narrow-mindedness?"

"I'm not a snob and it has nothing to do with being narrow-minded and everything to do with knowing who the Clayborn family is and what they represent. I want no part of that world again."

"Once again, I think I have been insulted. Do you know me or my family well enough to have that opinion? What have we done to you?" His tone had roughened with each sentence. "I think I deserve to hear you expound on that statement."

"Well, you're going to be disappointed."

Mark's brows came together over his nose.

"Instead, why don't you tell me what has you living on this side of the bay when I know the other side is thought to be the correct one?"

He placed some hot dog buns on the counter. "I needed a place to stay when I moved back and no one was staying in the summer house. It's no big mystery."

"That's right. I remember hearing talk that you were in a bad accident and left town afterwards."

He winced. "Yeah, I left to do my fellowship in California."

"Well, do tell. I am surprised. I would have never thought a Clayborn would live anywhere but Mobile."

"And for your information, my brother and I both moved away. I came back because my father had a stroke and needs someone close."

"I'm sorry to hear about your father." And she was. It was tough to see someone suffer that way. She remembered Mr. Clayborn, Sr. being a larger-than-life man whom everyone noticed when he came into the room. Much like Mark. She admired Mark for giving up his life in California to return home to care for his father. In comparison, she lived in the same town and didn't even speak to her parents.

"He had a bad stroke but he is recovering. Working every day is over for him but at least he's alive."

"Mommy," Allie called. "I'm hungry."

Mark shrugged. "I guess we'd better save this conversation for later. If you really want to help, why don't you get the plates and things together while I get these hot dogs on the grill? The plates are in that cabinet—" he pointed to one to the right of the stove "—and the silverware is in that drawer." He indicated the one right in front of her. "Condiments in the refrigerator. What few there are." He went out the side door of the kitchen without another word.

What Mark didn't realize was that she was through having any type of conversation about her past. Why she'd told him so much she had no idea.

CHAPTER THREE

MARK STARTED THE gas grill and adjusted the flame, before placing the hot dogs on the wire rack above it. He glanced back into the house through the window of the door. He could just see Laura Jo moving around.

She had a real chip on her shoulder about the world in which they had been raised. For a moment there he'd thought she might open up and tell him why but then she'd shut down. Why did it matter to him anyway?

Maybe it was because for some reason he liked the brash, independent and absolutely beautiful woman, especially when she laughed. He couldn't get enough of that uninhibited embracing of life. Would she act that way in bed?

Whoa, that was not where he was headed. He didn't really know her and what he did know about her was that she'd sooner sink her teeth into him than allow him to kiss her.

Just what was going on between her and her family? He knew of the Herrons. They were good people but Laura Jo had certainly had a falling out with them. She hadn't even told Allie she had grandparents living in town. Who did that? It just didn't make sense.

He'd enjoyed his afternoon with the children. It had been tough to drive with them in the car but he'd done it. He'd had a taste of what it would be like to have a child in his life and he rather liked it. In fact, he liked it too much.

Laura Jo made another trip by the door. He jerked around when she called from the doorway, "Hey, do you need a platter for those?"

"Yeah." Why did he feel like he'd just been caught in someone else's business? What was going on between her and her family wasn't his problem.

"Where do I find it? I'll bring it to you."

She looked so appealing, framed by the door with the afternoon sun highlighting one side of her face. The urge to kiss her almost overwhelmed him. He'd like to prove that they weren't different in the areas that mattered. He had to say something to get rid of her until he regained his equilibrium. "Cabinet below the plates."

Laura Jo disappeared into the house again. A few minutes later she came out and stood beside him. Her head reached his shoulders. She was close enough that he smelled a hint of her floral shampoo but not near enough that they touched. He was aware of the fact that all he had to do was take a half step and her body would be next to his.

"You might want to turn those. They look like they're burning."

Great. He had been so focussed on her that he wasn't thinking about what he was doing. "So now you're going to come out here and start telling me how to cook my hot dogs. Do you like to be bossed?"

She took a step back. Her eyes turned serious. "No. I don't. I'm sorry." She moved to leave.

He caught her wrist. "Hey, I was just kidding. They're just hot dogs."

Laura Jo pulled her arm out of his grip. "I know. But I need to get us some drinks. I saw the glasses when I was looking for a bowl." With that she was gone.

This was a woman better left alone. She had more hang-ups than he did and, heaven knew, he had plenty.

Twenty minutes later, Allie and Jeremy were picnicking, as they called it, in front of the TV so they could watch another parade. Mark had persuaded Laura Jo to join him on the deck. This was what he remembered it being like when he'd been a kid. He liked having people around. Being part of a family. Could he ever have that again?

He and Laura Jo ate in silence for a while, but not a comfortable one. Mark worked to come up with a subject they could discuss. Finally, he asked, "So you remembered me from years ago, so why don't I remember you?"

She grinned. "Oh, I don't know. Maybe because the only person you saw was Ann Maria Clark."

He had the good grace to turn red. "Yeah, we were a hot item back then."

"That you were. There was no reason you'd see a simple lady-in-waiting."

His gaze met hers. Something about her tone

made him think she might have liked him to notice her. "You were in her court?"

She nodded. "I was."

"I can't believe it."

"Well, it's true."

"We were that close all those years ago and it took a skinned knee at a parade for us to get to know each other."

She fingered the hot dog. "Life can be strange like that."

"That it can."

"I thought you two would get married," Laura Jo said, more as a statement of fact than someone fishing for information.

"That had been the plan but things changed."

"That happens. Especially where people are concerned." She sounded as if she was speaking about herself more than him.

It was time to change the subject. "Have you and Jeremy's mom been friends for a long time?"

"No. We only met a few years ago."

Well, at least he was getting more than a one-word answer.

"She works at the hospital?"

Laura Jo gave him a speculative look. "Are you interested in her?"

"I'm just trying to make conversation. Maybe learn a little more about you."

Laura Jo placed her half-eaten hot dog on the plate in front of her. She looked at him from across the table for a second before saying, "We met at a group for mothers without partners. Her husband had died. We became friends, at first because we needed each other, then we found we liked each other."

"So she was there when you needed someone." He knew well what it was like to be alone and need someone to talk to. There had been no one when he'd arrived in LA. He had been lonely then and, come to think of it, he'd been lonely in Mobile at least up until the last week.

"Your parents weren't around?"

"No. Hers had died. Mine…well, that's another story. That's why Marsha and I are trying to open a house for mothers who are on their own."

"So how's that going?"

"The city has agreed to sell us a house at a good price that would be perfect but we're running out of time to raise the money."

"Maybe I could be of some help. Atone for my car."

"A check for three hundred thousand would be great." She grinned at him as if she was making a joke but he could see hope in her eyes.

He winced. "That would be my car and at least one or two more."

"I've seen you ride a bike." She grinned.

He threw back his head and laughed. "You'd make me resort to that to get your house?'

"I'd do almost anything. This chance might not come again."

She took a swallow of her drink as if her mouth had suddenly gone dry.

Why did that thought of her in bed, beneath him, pop into his head? He raised a brow.

Her eyes widened. A stricken look covered her face. "You know what I mean."

"I have an idea. We could go to the Krewe of Orion dance together. See some of our old friends. There should be plenty of people there willing to donate. All you'd have to do is get one to agree to support you and then the others would line up to help out."

"I don't think so."

"To going with me or that others would help?"

"To going."

"Do you mind if I ask why?" He caught her gaze.

"That's not my idea of a good time anymore."

What had brought on that remark? He pushed his plate away. "Well, this is a first. A woman who doesn't want to get dressed up and go to a party."

"Not all women like that sort of stuff."

"It's just one night. Attending with me isn't like going to the gallows." He chuckled. "I promise."

"It's still no, thank you." She pushed half of her leftover hot dog bun across the plate.

"Well, I guess you have other plans for the way you're going to get the money for the house. I'm sorry, I need my car. However, I'll make a donation to the cause."

As if she was all of a sudden concerned about sounding rude, she said, "I do appreciate you trying to help. I'll take you up on that." She stood with plate in hand. "I guess I better get the kids home to bed. They have school tomorrow."

Mark also gathered his plate and joined her as

she walked into the house. They found Allie and Jeremy on the couch, Gus snoring between them.

"I'll write that check and help you get them loaded," Mark said as he took her plate and walked into the kitchen. While there he wrote a check. When he returned, Laura Jo already had Allie in her arms. He scooped Jeremy up and followed her out of the house. They worked together to get each child in and secured.

Digging in his front pocket, he pulled out the check and handed it to Laura Jo.

Laura Jo read it. Her eyes widened. She looked at him. "Thank you. This is very generous."

"You're welcome."

"Also thanks for giving Allie today. I don't have much of a chance to do things like this for her."

"I didn't just do it for Allie." They walked around to the driver's door and Laura Jo opened it.

"I know Jeremy also had a good time."

"What about you?"

"Me?"

"Yeah. I was hoping you had a nice day, too."

"I did."

She acted as if it was a foreign idea that he

might be interested in her having a good time. "Good. Maybe we could do it again sometime. Just you and me."

"I've already told you. We have nothing in common."

"Nonsense. We have a lot in common. Our childhoods, medicine, parades and laughter. That's more than most people have." When she'd been teasing him about Gus there had been an easiness between them. He wanted to see if she was putting up the front he believed she was. To make her act on her attraction to him. He was tired of being dismissed by her. "I bet if you tried, you could find something you like about me. Maybe this could help."

He wrapped an arm around her waist and pulled her to him. She only had time to gasp before his lips found hers. She didn't react at first, which gave him time to taste her lips. Soft, warm and slightly parted. Then for the briefest of seconds she returned his kiss. His heart thumped against his ribs at the possibilities before her hands spread wide against his chest. She shoved him away, hard.

His hands fell to his sides.

"You had no right to do that," she hissed.

"I can't say that I'm sorry."

She slid behind the steering wheel and before she could close the door he said, "Goodnight, Laura Jo."

"It's more like goodbye." She slammed the door.

Not a chance. Mark watched her taillights disappear up his drive. They'd be seeing each other again if he had anything to say about it. She was the first woman he'd met who had him thinking about the possibilities of tomorrow, even when he shouldn't.

It intrigued him that she put up such a fight not to have anything to do with him. That was except for the moments she'd melted in his arms. Could he get her to linger there long enough to forget whatever stood between them? Long enough to make her appreciate something they might both enjoy?

Laura Jo couldn't remember the last time a man had kissed her, but it sure hadn't been anything near as powerful as the brief one Mark had just given her. Her hands shook on the steering wheel.

Why had he done it? Hadn't she made it clear to him that she didn't want to become involved with him? Had she been giving off a different signal?

It didn't matter why. It couldn't, wouldn't happen again. There couldn't be anything real between them anyway. When she did open up again to a man she would know him well. She wanted someone settled, who wouldn't leave town at any moment. Someone who cared nothing for being involved in Mobile society. From what she knew about Mark so far, he had none of those qualities.

The lights of the cars flickered across the water as she traveled over the low bay causeway back to Mobile.

Thinking about and fretting over Mark was a waste of time. Laura Jo fingered the check he had given her. It was literally a raindrop in a pond to what she needed. She had to find some way to raise the money needed to buy the house. There was also Allie to see about and her job to keep. Mark Clayborn hadn't been hers years ago and he wasn't hers now.

Mark, she'd already learned, was a man with a strong sense of who he was. If she let him into her life he might try to control it, like her father and Phil had. She needed a partner, a father for Allie, someone sturdy and dependable. Until that happened it was her job to make decisions about her life and Allie's. She would never again depend on a man or let him dictate to her.

Marsha was there to greet her when she pulled into the parking area of the apartment complex. She had to have been watching for them. Knowing Marsha, she'd want details of the afternoon and evening. When Laura Jo had called her earlier to inform her that they would be staying a little longer at Mark's for supper, her speculative tone had made Laura Jo feel like she needed to justify her decision.

She'd told Marsha, "Don't get any ideas. There's nothing going on here."

"Okay, if you say so." Marsha hadn't sounded convinced before she'd hung up.

Allie and Jeremy woke when she parked. They got out of the car, talking a mile a minute about the parade and Gus. Marsha grinned over their heads at Laura Jo. "Come in and tell me all about your visit to Dr. Clayborn's," Marsha said, as if to the children but Laura Jo had no doubt she meant her.

"There's not much to tell and the kids have school tomorrow." Laura Jo locked her car.

"I know they have school tomorrow but you can come in for a few minutes."

Laura Jo straightened. Marsha wouldn't let it go until she'd heard every detail but Laura Jo wouldn't be telling her about the kiss. The one that had shaken something awake in her. It wouldn't happen again, even if there was an occasion, which there wouldn't be. She doubted that her path and Mark's would cross again. They didn't even live on the same side of the bay.

Allie and Jeremy ran ahead on the way to Marsha's apartment. She and Marsha followed more slowly.

A few minutes later, Marsha set a glass of iced tea in front of Laura Jo and said, "Okay, spill."

"Mark let the kids dress up Gus, his dog."

"So you're on a first-name basis with the good doc now?"

Laura Jo rolled her eyes. It was starting. "He asked me to call him Mark and it seemed foolish not to."

Marsha nodded in a thoughtful way, as if she

didn't believe her friend's reasoning. "So what else did you do?"

"We went to the parade. Mark walked with the kids while I watched." She chuckled.

"What's that laugh for?"

"I was just thinking of the look on Mark's face when he showed up pulling a wagon with the kids and the dog in it he'd bought off a boy."

Marsha gave her a long look. "That sounds interesting."

"It was." Laura Jo launched into the story, her smile growing as she told it.

She ended up laughing and Marsha joined her.

"So you went back to his place?"

"I wish you'd stop saying 'so' like that and acting as if it was a date. The only reason I agreed to go was because Allie wanted to dress up the dog and be in the parade so badly."

"So..."

Laura Jo glared at her.

"You didn't enjoy yourself at all?" Marsha continued without paying Laura Jo any attention.

"I don't even like the guy."

"This is the most you've had to do with a man

since I've known you. I think you might be a little more interested in him than you want to admit."

"I think you're wrong." Laura Jo was going to see to it that it was the truth. "There's one more thing and I probably shouldn't tell you this, but he did ask me to the krewe dance."

"And you said no." Marsha said the words as a statement of a fact.

"I did. For more than one reason."

Marsha turned serious. "We could use his contacts."

"I've already told you that I'm not going to do that. What if I saw my parents and they found out I was there, asking for money. I couldn't face them like that."

"Even at the cost of losing the house? Laura Jo, you've been gone so long I can't imagine that your parents would see it as crawling back."

"You don't know my father. It would be his chance to tell me 'I told you so.' I lived though that once. Not again."

Marsha didn't know that Laura Jo hadn't spoken to her parents since before Allie's birth.

"So I guess we'll put all our hope in that grant coming through."

Laura Jo took a sip of her tea then said, "Yes, that and a moneybags willing to help us out."

"You've got a moneybag in Mark Clayborn."

"Oh, I forgot to show you this." Laura Jo pulled the check Mark had given her out of her pocket."

Marsha whistled. "Very generous. He must really like you."

"No. It was more like I made him feel guilty."

"Whatever you did, at least this will help. We just need to get others to be so kind."

"Now I'm not only indebted to him for giving Allie a wonderful afternoon but for helping with the shelter."

"You don't like that, do you, Ms. I-Can-Do-It-Myself?"

"No, I don't. We have nothing in common. He and I don't want the same things out of life anymore."

"Oh, and you know that by spending one afternoon with him?" Marsha picked up both of their glasses and placed them in the sink. "You do know that people with money also care about their families, love them, want the best for them?"

All of what Laura's Jo's father had said to her just before he'd told her that Phil was no good.

Had her father felt the same way about her as she did about Allie? Worry that something bad might happen to her? Worry over her happiness?

"Well, it's time for me to get Allie home."

As Laura Jo and Allie made their way to the front door Marsha said, "We've got to find that money for the shelter. There are worse things in life to have to do than dress up and go out with a handsome man to a dance."

"What handsome man, Mama?"

"No one, honey. Aunt Marsha is just trying to be funny."

Mark was handsome. But what Laura Jo was more concerned about was the way his kiss had made her feel. Had made her wish for more.

Mark came out of a deep sleep at the ringing of his cell phone.

What time was it? He checked his bedside clock. 3:00 a.m. This was never good news. Had something happened to his father?

Mark snatched up the phone. "Hello."

"Mark, its Laura Jo."

The relief that he felt that the call wasn't about

his father was immediately replaced with concern for her.

"I'm sorry to call…"

He was wide awake now, heart throbbing. "Are you all right? Allie?"

"Yes. Yes. We're fine. It's a child staying at the shelter. The mother has no insurance and is afraid of doctors. I think the child needs to be seen. Fever, sweating, not eating and lethargic. The mother won't agree to go to the hospital. Will you come?"

"Sure, but will she let me examine the child if I do?"

"I'll convince her that it's necessary before you get here. If she wants to stay at the shelter then she'll have to let you."

"Give me directions."

Laura Jo gave him an address in a less-than-desirable area of the city.

"I'll be there in about thirty minutes."

"Thanks, Mark. I really appreciate this."

The longest part of the trip was traveling the two-lane road between his house and the interstate. Even at this early hour it took him more time than he would have liked. Finally, he reached the four-lane, where he could speed across the two-mile causeway that bisected the bay.

The child must really be worrying Laura Jo or she would never have called him. She'd made it clear she didn't plan to see him again when she'd left his house. He'd thought of nothing but their kiss for the rest of the evening. To hear her voice on the other end of the phone had been a surprise. The child's symptoms didn't sound all that unusual but with a small person it wasn't always straightforward.

He drove through the tunnel that went under Mobile River and came up on Governor Street. There were no crowds now, only large oaks and barriers lining the main street. A number of miles down the street he made a left and not long after that he pulled up in front of what looked like a building that had been a business at one time. The glass windows were painted black and there were dark curtains over the door window. One lone light burned above it. It looked nothing like a place for pregnant woman or children. He could clearly see why they needed a house to move to.

Laura Jo's car was parked near the door and he took the slot next to hers. Picking up his cell phone, he pressed Return. Seconds later, Laura Jo's voice came on the line. "I'm outside."

"I'll be right there."

Mark stood at the door for only seconds before the dead bolt clicked back and Laura Jo's face came into view.

After making sure it was him, she opened the door wider. "I appreciate you coming."

He entered and she locked the door behind him. The room he was in resembled a living room with its couches and chairs spread out. There was one small TV in the corner. At least it looked more welcoming from the inside than it did from the outside.

"Anna's family's room is down this way." Laura Jo, dressed in jeans, T-shirt and tennis shoes, led him down a hall toward the back of the building, passing what he guessed had once been offices. Were families living in nothing more than ten-by-ten rooms?

"Has anything changed?" Mark asked.

"No, but I'm really worried. Anna has been so distraught about the loss of her husband I'm not sure she's been as attentive to her children as she should have been."

"I'll have a look and see what we come up with. Don't worry."

They stopped at the last door.

"Anna isn't a fan of doctors."

"I'll be on my best behavior." He gave her a reassuring smile.

Laura Jo nodded and knocked quietly on the door before she opened it. "Anna, someone is here to check on little Marcy."

Laura Jo entered and he followed close behind. A lone light shone, barely giving off enough light for him to see the room. There was a twin bed shoved into the corner and another at a right angle to that one where two children slept feet to feet. There was also a baby bed but it was empty because the child was in her mother's arms. The woman was reed thin, wide-eyed and had wavy hair. She couldn't have been more than twenty-five.

"Hi, Anna, I'm Mark, and I've come to see if I can help little Marcy. Why don't you sit on the bed and hold her while I have a look? I promise not to hurt her."

Anna hesitated then looked a Laura Jo.

"I'll sit beside you." Laura Jo led her over to the bed.

Mark went down on one knee and placed his bag beside him. He pulled out his stethoscope. The heat he felt as he put his hand close to the child's chest indicated she was still running a fever.

"I'm only going to listen to her heart and lungs now. Check her pulse." He gave the mother a reassuring smile and went to work. Done, he asked, "How long has she had this fever?"

"Since yesterday," the mother said in a meek voice.

He looked a Laura Jo.

"I had no idea." She sounded defensive and he hadn't intended to make her feel that.

To Anna he said, "I'm going to need to check Marcy's abdomen."

"Let's lay Marcy on the bed. That way she'll be more comfortable," Laura Jo suggested.

Mark moved his hand over the child's stomach area. It was distended and hard. Something serious was, without a doubt, going on. He glanced at Laura Jo. Their gazes met. The worry in her eyes was obvious.

"Anna, thank you for letting me see Marcy." He looked at Laura Jo again and tilted his head toward the door. As he stood he picked up his bag and walked across the room. Laura joined him. He let her precede him into the hall and closed the door behind him.

Laura Jo looked at him.

"Marcy has to go to the hospital."

"I was afraid of that. What do you think the problem is?"

"The symptoms make me think it might be an obstructive bowel problem. This isn't something that can wait. Marcy must been seen at the hospital."

"I'll talk to her." Laura Jo went back into the room.

Mark pulled out his phone and called the ER. He gave the information about Marcy and they assured him they would be ready when he arrived. Finished, he leaned against the wall to wait.

Soon Laura Jo came out, with Anna holding Marcy in her arms.

"Anna has agreed to go to the hospital as long as you and I stay with her," Laura Jo said. "I need a few minutes to let someone know to see about her other children. Will you drive?"

His stomach tightened. He didn't want to but what was he supposed to say, "No, I might injure you for life"?

"If it's necessary," Mark answered.

Laura Jo looked at him with a question in her eyes before he turned to walk down the hallway to the front.

"The car seat is by the front door," Anna said in a subdued voice.

"I'll get it."

He was still working to latch the child seat into his car when Laura Jo arrived.

"I'll get that."

With efficiency that he envied she had the seat secured and Marcy in it in no time. Laura Jo didn't comment on his ineptness but he was sure she'd made a note of it. She would probably call him on it later.

Anna took the backseat next to Marcy, and Laura Jo joined him in front. Before pulling out of the parking space, he looked back to see that the baby was secure and that Anna was wearing her seat belt. "Are you buckled in, Laura Jo?"

"Yes. You sure are safety conscious."

Yes, he was, and he had a good reason to be. Mark nodded and wasted no time driving to the hospital. He pulled under the emergency awning and stopped.

As they entered the building Laura Jo said to Anna, "We'll be right here with you until you feel comfortable. They'll take good care of Marcy here."

Anna nodded, her eyes not meeting Laura Jo's.

They were met by a woman dressed in scrubs.

"Lynn, this child needs to be seen," Laura said.

"Is this the girl Dr. Clayborn called in about?"

"Yes," he said. "I'm Dr. Clayborn." Because he wasn't on the staff at the hospital he couldn't give orders. They would have to wait until the ER physician showed up.

"Exam room five is open. Dr. Lawrence will be right in."

Two hours later Marcy was in surgery. Mark's diagnosis had been correct. Thankfully, Laura Jo had called him or the child might have died. They were now sitting in the surgery waiting room with Anna. With Laura Jo's support, Anna had accepted that Marcy needed the surgery. Mark was impressed with the tender understanding Laura Jo had given the terrified mother. He liked this sensitive side of her personally. What would it take for her to turn some of that on him?

Mark approached the two women and handed each one a cup of coffee from the machine. He slipped into the chair beside Laura Jo. Waiting in hospitals wasn't his usual activity. He'd always been on the working end of an emergency.

While Anna was in the restroom Laura Jo said, "I think you can go. She seems to be handling this better than I thought she would."

"No, I said I'd stay and I will."

"You make a good friend."

Mark's chest tightened. No, he didn't. He'd already proved that. Mike certainly wouldn't say that about him. Mark hadn't even gone to the hospital to see Mike before he'd left town. Laura Jo shouldn't start depending on him.

"You might be surprised."

Laura Jo gave him a speculative look but he was saved from any questions by Anna returning. Soon after that the surgeon came out to speak to them.

The sun was shining when he and Laura Jo

stepped outside the hospital. Marcy was doing well in PICU and Anna had insisted that she was fine and no longer needed them there. They left her in the waiting room, dozing. Laura Jo had promised to check on her other children and that she would see to it they were cared for properly.

As he and Laura Jo walked to his car, which he had moved to a parking place earlier, Mark asked, "Where do you get all the energy for all you do?"

"I just do what has to be done."

"You sure have a lot on your plate."

"Maybe so, but some things I can't say no to."

What was it like to feel that type of bond with people? He understood the practical side of doing what needed to be done medically to save a life but it was a completely different concept to support another person emotionally without reservation. Mark understood that well. He hadn't been able to stand beside his best friend when he'd needed him most. He had even ignored his conscience when it had screamed for him to do better. It hadn't gotten quieter when he'd moved back to town but he still couldn't muster the guts to go visit Mike.

"I wish I had your backbone."

"How's that?"

"You face life head-on."

"You don't?"

"What little I have falls short of the amount you have."

"Thank you. That's a nice compliment."

They had reached his car. "How about I buy us some breakfast then take you home? I'm guessing Marsha has Allie."

"Yes. I really need to check on her and Anna's kids. I need sleep. I'm sure you do also. I have to work this afternoon. Don't you have to be at work this morning?"

"I don't go in until two and you need to eat. I'm hungry so why don't you let me get us some breakfast without disagreeing for once?"

She walked to the passenger door. "I'm already too far in debt to you."

"I don't mind that."

She sighed. "I pick the place."

"Ladies choice, then."

A smile spread across her lips. "I like the sound of that."

Had no one ever let her make a choice of where

they went? He liked seeing Laura Jo smile. She didn't do it often enough. She was far too serious.

"Where're we going?"

"I'll show you."

She got in the car and put her seat belt on. When he was ready to pull out he looked over at her.

Laura Jo said, "Yes, I have buckled up."

He had to sound crazy to her, or over-the-top controlling, but he just couldn't face hurting someone with his driving ever again. Somehow it seemed easier when he had her in the car with him; she accepted him for who he was. As he drove she gave him directions into an older and seedier part of downtown Mobile. He had last been to the area when he'd been a teen and trying to live on the wild side some.

"It's just down the street on the right. The Silver Spoon."

Mark pulled into the small parking area in front of a nineteen-fifties-style café that had seen better days.

"You want to eat here?"

"Sure. They have the best pecan waffles in town." Laura Jo was already getting out of the car. She looked back in at him. "You coming?"

Mark had been questioning it. He wasn't sure the place could pass a health inspection.

"Yes, I am." He climbed out of the car. "I wouldn't miss it."

She was already moving up the few steps to the front door.

Because all the booths were full, Laura Jo took an empty stool at the bar. She didn't miss Mark's dubious look at the duct-taped stool next to her before he took a seat.

"You don't frequent places like this, do you?"

"I can say that this is a first."

She grinned. "I thought it might be."

Mark picked up a plastic-covered menu. "So I need to have the pecan waffles."

"They're my favorite." She was going to enjoy watching Mark out of his element.

"Then waffles it is. You do the ordering."

"Charlie," she said to the heavy man wearing what once must have been a white apron, "we'll have pecan waffles, link sausage and iced tea."

"Coming right up, Laura Jo," Charlie said, and turned to give the cook her order.

"I see you're a regular," Mark said.

"I come when I can, which isn't often enough."

Charlie put their glasses of iced tea on the counter with a thump.

"I don't normally have iced tea for breakfast." Mark picked up his glass.

"If you'd rather have coffee…" Laura Jo made it sound like a dare on purpose.

"I said I wanted the same as you and that's what I'm having. So how did you find this place?"

"Charlie gave one of the mothers that came through the shelter a job here after her baby was born."

"That was nice. I'm impressed with what you're doing at the shelter."

"Thanks. But it never seems like enough. You know, I really appreciate you helping me out with Anna and Marcy. I hated to call you but I knew I couldn't get her to the hospital and I was uncomfortable with how Marcy looked."

Mark really had been great with Anna and Marcy. He'd stayed to give moral support even when he hadn't had to. Maybe she had better character radar than she believed.

"I'm glad you thought you could call."

She'd been surprised too that she hadn't hesitated a second before picking up the phone to call him. Somehow she'd just known he would come. "Were you always going to be a doctor?"

"I believe that's the first personal question you have ever asked me. You do want to get to know me better."

Laura Jo opened her mouth to refute that statement but he continued, not giving her a chance to do so.

"Yes, I had always planned to go into medicine. My parents liked the idea and I found I did, too. I've always liked helping people. How about you? Did you always dream of being a nurse?"

"No, I kind of came to that later in life."

"So what was your dream?"

"I don't know. I guess like all the other girls I knew we dreamed of marrying the Mardi Gras king, having two kids and living in a big house."

He looked in her direction but she refused to meet his gaze. "Marrying the Mardi Gras king, was it? So did you dream of marrying me?"

"I don't think your ego needs to be fed by my teenage dreams. But I'll admit to having a crush on you if that will end this conversation."

"I thought so."

"Now we won't be able to get your head out of the door."

Charlie placed a plateful of food in front of each of them with a clunk on the counter.

"Thanks, Charlie." She picked up her fork and looked at Mark. "You need to eat your waffle while it's hot to get the full effect." She took a bite dripping with syrup.

"Trying to get me to quit asking questions?"

"That and the waffles are better hot."

They ate in silence for a few minutes.

"So I remember something about an accident and then I didn't hear much about you after that. I later heard you'd left town. Did you get hurt?"

Mark's fork halted in midair then he lowered it to the plate.

Had she asked the wrong thing? She looked back at her meal. "You don't have to tell me if you'd rather not."

"I wasn't really hurt. But my friend was. I had to leave a few days later to start my fellowship."

"What happened?"

"It's a long story. Too much of one for this morning."

So the man with all the questions was hiding

something. Minutes later she finished her last mouthful. Mark said something. She turned to look at him. "What?"

He touched her face. His gaze caught and held hers as he put his finger between his lips. Her stomach fluttered. She swallowed. Heaven help her, the man held her spellbound.

"You had syrup on your chin."

"Uh?"

"Syrup on your chin." Mark said each word slowly, as if speaking to someone who didn't understand the language.

"Oh." She dabbed at the spot with her napkin. Mark was starting to shatter her protective barriers. "We'd better go."

She climbed off the stool and called, "Thanks, Charlie." She was going out the door as Mark pulled a couple of bills out of his wallet.

Her hand was already on the door handle of his car as Mark pulled into a parking place at the shelter. She needed to get away from him. Find her equilibrium. That look in his eye as he'd licked the syrup on his finger had her thinking of things better left unthought. She stepped out of the car. "Thanks for helping out last night. I don't know how I'll repay you."

"No problem."

"Bye, Mark."

Why did a simple gesture from Mark, of all men, make her run? She had to be attracted to him for that to happen. Surely that wasn't the case.

CHAPTER FOUR

FOUR DAYS LATER, as Laura Jo was busy setting up the med tent on North Broad Street, she was still pondering how to raise the money needed for the single mothers' shelter. The grant they were hoping for had come through, but with a condition that the board match the amount. There were only five more days of Mardi Gras season, then things would settle down. After that the city would place the house on the market. She couldn't let that happen. They had to move out of the too-small building they were in now.

She didn't want anyone to get hurt at the parade but if she was busy tonight it would keep her mind off the issue of money...along with the thoughts of how agreeing to go to the dance with Mark just might solve her problem.

Think of the devil and he shows up. Mark rode over the curb of the street and up onto the grassy lot where the med tent was stationed. His tight bike shorts left little to the imagination and there was nothing small about the man. He unclipped his helmet and set it on the handlebars, before heading in her direction. For a second her heart rate picked up with the thought that he'd come to see her. She wasn't sure if it was relief or disappointment that filled her when he stopped to talk in depth to one of the ER doctors working with her. Mark should mean nothing to her. She shouldn't be feeling anything, one way or another.

Laura Jo returned to unpacking boxes, turning her back to him.

A few minutes later a tenor voice she recognized said, "Hello, Laura Jo."

She twisted, making an effort to act as if she hadn't been aware of where he'd been and what he'd been doing during the past ten minutes. "Hi, Mark. I didn't expect to see you today."

"It would be my guess that if you had you'd have seen to it you were reassigned to another med tent."

"You know me so well," she quipped, returning to what she'd been doing.

"I wish I did know you better. Then maybe I'd understand why I find you so fascinating."

A ripple of pleasure went through her at his statement. She resisted placing a hand on her stomach when it quivered. "It might be that I don't fall at your feet like other women do."

"I don't know about that."

"They used to. I figured now wasn't any different. In fact, I saw and heard the ER nurses swoon when you came in the other day."

"Swoon. That's an old-fashioned word." He leaned in close so that only she could hear. "Did you swoon over me, too, Laura Jo?"

She had but she wasn't going to let him know that. Straightening and squaring her shoulders, she said with authority, "I did not."

He grinned, his voice dropping seductively. "Something about that quick denial makes me think you did."

Her heart skipped a beat. "Would you please go? I have work to do."

He chuckled. "I'm flattered. I had no idea girls swooned over me."

I bet. Laura Jo glared at him.

"I'm going. I wouldn't want to keep you from your work. See you later."

She glanced up to see him disappear through the crowd. Their conversations had been the most thought-provoking, irritating and stimulating ones she'd ever experienced. And that didn't count how he'd made her feel when he'd kissed her. She had to think fast to stay ahead of him. Somehow that made her life more exciting and interesting.

Mark made one more circle around his patrol area along the parade route. He'd not worked patrol in three days and his muscles were telling him they had noticed. Busy at his practice, getting his patient load up, it required late hours to accommodate people coming in after work hours. As the newest man in the six-doctor general practice, it was his duty to cover the clinic for the hours that were least desirable.

He was pulled out of his thoughts by a boy of three or four standing in the middle of the street. The child looked lost. Mark parked his bike and scanned the crowd for some anxious parent. Finding none, he went down on his haunches in front of the boy. "Hello, there, are you looking for someone?"

"My mommy."

"Can I help you find her?"

The boy nodded.

Mark offered his hand and he took it. They started walking along the edge of the crowd, Mark looking for anyone who might claim the boy.

A woman clutching her cell phone stepped out from behind the barriers just ahead of them and hurried toward them. "Lucas, you shouldn't have walked off."

The woman looked at Mark. "I was talking on my phone and then he was gone," she said with a nervous little laugh.

Mark nodded. "I understand. Little ones can get away from you when you aren't paying attention."

The woman's lips tightened. She took her son's hand and left.

He went back to patrolling. Returning to Mobile so close to Mardi Gras season, he had social obligations to consider. He'd been king the year he'd left and now that he was back in town he was expected to attend certain events. He'd once lived for all the fanfare of the season but now it held no real thrill for him. Still, certain things were expected of him. He just wished doing so didn't bring on such heavy guilt.

Mark hadn't expected to find Laura Jo working the same parade as he was but he wasn't disappointed either. He'd missed their sparring. It was always fun to see how she'd react to something he said or did. Especially his kiss. He'd kissed enough women to know when one was enjoying it.

He wasn't disappointed with her reaction today, either. When he'd asked her about swooning over him he'd have to admit her pretty blush had raised his self-esteem. She had been one of those teens who'd wanted to be noticed by him. The sad thing was that he would've crushed her admiration with the self-centered attitude he'd wore like his royal cloak if he'd even noticed her.

Clearly he had noted the woman she'd become. There hadn't been another female who kept him on his toes or stepped on them more than she did. There were so many facets to her. He still didn't understand what made her tick. He couldn't count the number of times she'd been on his mind over the past few days despite his efforts not to let her intervene in his thoughts.

He compared the mother who'd been too busy talking on her phone to show any real concern for her child with Laura Jo's motherly concern over a skinned knee. She won. Laura Jo had seen the humor when he'd had to carry Gus. He could still hear her boisterous laughter. Under all that anti-society, I-can-do-it-on-my-own attitude, she hid a power to love and enjoy life.

From what he'd heard and read between the lines, she hadn't had much opportunity to take pleasure in life in a number of years. She been busy scrapping and fighting to keep Allie cared for. To go to school, then work and start a shelter. It had to have been hard, doing it all without family support. What was the deal with her family anyway?

No wonder she was so involved with the single mothers' house. She identified with the women, had been one of them. As if she didn't have enough going on in her life now, she was trying to raise funds to buy the house. Was there anything Laura Jo couldn't do?

Mark made another loop through his section of the parade route. He wasn't far from the med tent when he pulled over out of the way to let the parade go by. One girl in a group of dancers he recognized from other parades. She was limping badly. Seconds later, the girl left the line and collapsed to the curb.

To help her, he had to cross the parade route. He raised his hand and the driver of the next float stopped. Mark pushed his bike over to where the teenage girl sat. She was busy removing her tap shoe. Mark noticed that her foot was covered in blood.

He parked his bike and crouched beside her. The girl looked at him with tears in her eyes. "I just couldn't go any further."

It wasn't unusual to see members of the dance groups abusing their feet. Some of the dancers did up to four parades a day when it got closer to Fat Tuesday. More than once Mark had wondered how they kept it up. Almost everyone in the parades rode while these girls danced for miles.

"I don't blame you. That looks painful. How about we get you cleaned up and ease that pain?"

The girl nodded then started to stand. Mark

picked up her discarded shoe and placed his hand on her shoulder. "The med tent isn't too far. Do you mind if I carry you? That foot looks too painful to walk on."

The girl nodded. Mark handed her the shoe and scooped her into his arms. The crowd parted so he could get through. "Would someone please follow us with my bike?"

A middle-aged man called, "I'll bring it."

Mark headed for the med tent a block away. As he walked people turned to watch. He was within sight of the tent when he saw Laura Jo look in his direction. It was as if she had radar where he was concerned. She seemed to sense when he was near. He would have to give that more thought later. He hefted the girl closer in his arms. This was turning into a workout.

Laura Jo moved away and when he saw her again she was pushing a wheelchair across the dirt and grass area between them. Mark faltered. The girl's arms tightened around his neck. The blood drained from his face as Mike crossed his mind.

When Laura Jo reached him, he lowered the dancer into the chair.

Laura Jo mouthed over the girl's head, "Are you okay?"

He nodded. But the look on her face had him doubting he'd convinced her.

"What happened?"

"Blisters."

"I'll get things ready." Laura Jo turned and hurried back toward the tent.

Mark let his hands rest on the handles of the chair for a moment before he started pushing. He wished he could have let Laura Jo do it. Bringing the wheelchair up on its two back wheels, he maneuvered it across the rough ground. When he arrived at the tent Laura Jo was waiting with a square plastic pan filled with what must be saline. He lifted the footrest off the chair. Going on one knee, he removed the girl's other tap shoe. Laura Jo then slipped the pan into position and the girl lowered her feet into the water with a small yelp of pain.

"Do it slowly and it will be less painful. It'll hurt at first but as soon as they are clean we'll bandage them and you'll feel a lot better. Are you allergic to anything?"

"No," the girl said.

Laura Jo then offered her a white pill and a small glass of water that had been waiting on the table beside them. "That should ease the pain." She looked at him. "I'll take care of her from here, Dr. Clayborn."

Had he just been dismissed? He had. Grinning at Laura Jo and then the girl, he said, "I'll leave you in the capable hands of Nurse Akins."

"Thank you," the girl said.

"You're welcome. I hope you get to feeling better. I'll miss seeing you in the parades."

The girl blushed a bright pink then looked away.

Laura Jo gave a dramatic roll of her eyes.

Mark smiled. He looked around to find his bike leaning against a nearby tree. He climbed on and prepared to ride off. He glanced back at Laura Jo. She looked away from caring for the girl's feet to meet his gaze.

He grinned. Maybe he could still make her swoon.

Two hours later, after the last parade of the day, he pulled up beside the med tent. He would leave his reports of the minor injuries he'd handled with them. The city officials liked to keep a record of anything that happened during Mardi Gras season in order to plan for the next year.

Allie came running toward him. "Hey, did you bring Gus with you?"

"No, not today. I couldn't get him to ride the bike."

Allie giggled.

"Had any king cake this week?"

Allie nodded. "I even found the baby."

"Then I guess you're planning to take a cake to school."

"We're out of school today. It's our Mardi Gras break."

"Well, then, how about bringing me one? I haven't even had the chance to find the baby this year."

Laura Jo walked over "I don't think—"

Mark looked at her. "It just so happens that your mother owes me a favor."

"I do?"

"Anna."

Laura Jo's heart fell. She did.

"So how about you and your mother come over to my house tomorrow night and I'll fix sausage gumbo and you bring the king cake. Better yet, your mother can make it at my house." He looked at Laura Jo when he said, "She did say my kitchen was the perfect place to make a cake."

"Can we, Mommy? I want to see Gus. You don't have to work tomorrow."

"Great. Then it's all settled. I'll expect you at four o'clock."

"Do you two think I could say something since you're making plans that involve me?"

Mark looked at her and grinned. "Talk away."

"Allie, I think we need to take it easy while we have a day off. The next few days are going to be busy."

Mark leaned forward, making eye contact. "And I think that you owe me a favor that you are trying to welch on."

Laura Jo shifted from one foot to the other. She did owe him big for helping her with Anna, and the check, and Allie being in the parade. Even so, going to Mark's house again wasn't a good idea. "I thought you might be enough of a gentleman that you wouldn't stoop to calling in a favor."

He gave her a pointed look. "Sometimes you

want something badly enough that the social graces don't matter."

She swallowed. The implication was that she might be that "something." When had been the last time she'd felt wanted by a man? It had been so long ago she couldn't remember.

Mark looked at Allie and grinned. "Manners don't matter when you're talking about king cake."

Allie returned the smile and nodded.

Why was she letting Mark talk her into it? Because the least she owed him was a king cake for all that he'd done for her. And she had to admit that deep down inside she'd enjoy cooking in his kitchen and spending time with him.

Mark couldn't remember the last time he'd looked forward to a king cake with such anticipation. He suspected that it had nothing to do with the cake and everything to do with seeing Laura Jo. She and Allie were due any minute. He gave the gumbo a stir. He'd missed the stew-type consistency of the dish while he'd been in California. As hard as he'd tried, he hadn't been able to get the ingredients to make good gumbo. What he had used had never tasted like what he was used to having when he was in Mobile.

He slurped a spoonful of gumbo off the tip of the ladle. It was good.

The doorbell rang. Should a man be so eager to spend time with a woman? For his own self-preservation he'd say no. With a smile on his face, Mark opened the door. To his amazement, Laura Jo smiled in return. He hadn't expected that when he'd given her no choice about coming to his home today. Allie brushed passed his legs.

"Where's Gus?" she asked as she went.

"He was in his bed, sleeping, the last time I saw him."

He liked Allie. He'd never spent much time around children but he found Allie a pleasure. She seemed to like him as much as he did her. What would it be like to be a father to a child like her? Maybe if he had Allie as a daughter he'd have a chance of being a good father.

"I hope Gus is prepared for this," Laura Jo said.

"I wouldn't worry about Gus. Can I take those?" He reached for the grocery bags she carried in either hand.

"Thanks." She handed him one of them. "I guess I'd better get started. It's a long process."

It occurred to him that she'd be anxious to get away as soon as she had met her obligation. He didn't plan to let that happen. "We have plenty of time. I have nowhere to be tonight—do you?"

"Uh, no, but I'd still like to get started."

"Okay, if that's the way you want it." To his astonishment, he said, "I'm going to take Gus and Allie outside to play. Gus needs some exercise." When had he started to think that he was capable of overseeing Allie?

"All right. Just don't let Allie get too close to the water."

"I'll take good care of her." He was confident he would. He headed in the direction of the living room.

Laura Jo watched as Mark left the kitchen after he'd placed the bag on the kitchen counter. He headed out as if he'd given her no more thought. For some reason, she was disappointed he'd not worked harder at encouraging her to join him and Allie. She was even more surprised that she trusted him without question to take care of Allie.

Was it because she'd seen him caring for others or that she just innately knew he would see to Allie like she was his own?

Running a hand over the granite counter, she looked around the kitchen. It was truly amazing. If she had this kitchen to cook in every day, she might never leave it. But she didn't. What she had was a small corner one and it was plenty for her and Allie. Mark's kitchen reminded her of her childhood when she'd stood beside Elsie Mae, their cook, and helped prepared meals.

It was time to get busy. She planned to make the most of Mark's kitchen while she had it. Shaking off the nostalgia, Laura Jo pulled the bread flour and eggs out of the bag she'd brought. Over the next twenty minutes she prepared the dough and set it aside to rise.

Going to one of the living-room windows, she looked out. Allie was running with Gus as Mark threw a ball. Laura Jo laughed. Gus showed no interest in going after the ball. Seconds later Mark opened his arms wide and Allie ran into them. He lifted her over his head. Laura Jo could hear her daughter's giggles from where she stood. Her chest tightened.

Allie wrapped her arms around Mark's neck as he brought her back down. They both had huge smiles on their faces. Laura Jo swallowed the lump in her throat. The man had obviously won her daughter over and Laura Jo was worried he was fast doing the same with her.

She pulled open the door and walked out to join them. Allie and Mark were so absorbed in playing that they didn't see her until she had almost reached them. Seeing Allie with Mark brought home how much Allie needed a male figure in her life. Had she done Allie a disservice by not looking for a husband or keeping her away from her grandfather? Had she been so wrapped up in surviving and trying to take care of other mothers that she'd neglected Allie's needs?

"Is something wrong?" Mark asked.

"No, everything is fine."

"You had a funny look on your face. Was there a problem in the kitchen?"

"No, I found what I needed. Now I have to wait for the dough to rise before I do anything more."

"Then why don't we walk down to the dock?" Mark suggested.

"Okay."

"Come on, Allie," Mark called.

"So, do you boat or water-ski?" Laura Jo asked.

Mark stopped and looked at her. "You know, I like you being interested in me."

"Please, don't make more of a friendly question than there is. I was just trying to make conversation. You live on the water, were raised on the water so I just thought…"

"Yes, I have a small sailboat and the family also has a ski boat."

She and Mark walked to the end of the pier and took a seat in the Adirondack chairs stationed there.

"How about you?" he asked.

"I don't sail but I do love to ski." She watched the small waves coming in as the wind picked up.

"Maybe you and Allie can come and spend the day on the water with me when it gets warmer."

Allie ran past them to the edge of the pier.

"Be careful," Mark called. "The water is cold. I don't want you to fall in."

"You sure do sound like a parent."

Mark took on a stricken look that soon turned thoughtful. "I did, didn't I?"

"I don't know why you should act so surprised. You're great with kids."

A few minutes went by before he asked, "I know who your parents are but I can't remember if you have any brothers or sisters."

"Only child." Laura Jo wasn't pleased he'd turned the conversation to her and even less so to her parents. She didn't want to talk about them. The people who had been more interested in their social events than spending time with her. Who hadn't understood the teen who'd believed so strongly in helping the less fortunate. Who had always made her feel like she didn't quite measure up.

"Really? That wouldn't have been my guess."

"Why not?"

"Because you're so strong and self-sufficient. You don't seem spoiled to me."

"You do have a stereotypical view of an only child."

He shrugged. "You could be right."

Laura Jo kept an eye on Allie, who had left the pier and was now playing along the edge of the water as Gus lumbered along nearby.

"So tell me about growing up as a Clayborn with a big silver spoon in your mouth."

"I had no silver spoon that I can remember."

She gave him a sideways look. "I remember enough to know you were the golden boy."

"Well, I do have blond locks." Mark ran his hand through his hair with an attitude.

"And an ego."

They watched the water for a while before she stood and called to Allie, "Do you want to help braid the dough?"

"I want to do the colors," Allie said.

"Okay, I'll save that job for you."

Laura Jo headed back along the pier and Mark followed a number of paces behind her. As she stepped on the lawn her phone rang. Fishing it out of her jeans pocket, she saw it was Marsha calling and answered.

"Hey, I've just been given tickets to see that new kids' movie. Jeremy wants Allie to go with him. Would you mind if I come and get her?"

"I don't know, Marsha…" If she agreed, it would leave her alone with Mark.

"You mean you'd keep your child from seeing a movie she's been wanting to see because you're too afraid to stay by yourself with Mark Clayborn."

Put that way, it did sound kind of childish. But it was true.

After a sigh Laura Jo said, "Let me speak to Allie. She may rather stay here with the dog."

Laura Jo called to her daughter. Hearing the idea, Allie jumped up and down, squealing that she wanted to go to the movie.

"Okay, Marsha, but you'll have to come and get her. I'm in the middle of making king cakes."

"I'll be there in thirty minutes."

While they waited for Marsha to arrive, Laura Jo punched the dough down and placed it in the refrigerator to rest. She then cleaned Allie up so she'd be ready to go when Marsha arrived.

"Who's going to hide the baby if you leave?" Mark teased Allie.

"I bet Mommy will let you."

He looked over at Laura Jo. "Will you?"

"Yes, you can hide the baby." She made it sound like she was talking to a mischievous boy.

"Mark, will you do the colors for me too?" Allie asked, as she pulled on one of Gus's ears.

"I don't know if I know how to do those." Mark

was sitting in a large chair in the living area with one foot on the ottoman.

"Mommy will show you. She knows how to do it all."

Mark met Laura Jo's gaze over Allie's head. "She knows how to do it all, does she?"

A tingle went down her spine. Leave it to Mark to make baking a king cake sound sexier than it really was.

Five minutes later there was a knock at the door. Allie skipped to it while Laura Jo and Mark followed behind her. Laura Jo stepped around Allie and opened the door.

"Come on, Allie," Marsha said. "We need to hurry if we're going to be there on time." Marsha looked at Laura Jo. "Just let her spend the night since she was coming to me early in the morning anyway. Enjoy your evening. Hi, Mark. Bye, Mark." With that, Marsha whisked Allie away.

"Does she always blow in and blow out with such force?" Mark asked.

Laura Jo closed the door with a heavy awareness of being alone with Mark. "Sometimes. I need to finish the cake and get out of your way."

"I invited you to dinner and I expect you to

stay. Are you scared to be here with me, knowing Allie isn't here to protect you?"

"She wasn't protecting me!" Had she been using Allie as a barrier between her and men? No, her first priority was Allie and taking care of her. It had nothing to do with fear.

"Then quit acting as if you're scared I might jump you."

Laura Jo ignored his comment and headed toward the kitchen. She pulled the large bowl of dough out of the refrigerator.

"So what has to be done to it now?" Mark asked.

"Roll it out." She placed the bowl on the corner. "Will you hand me that bag of flour?"

He reached across the wide counter and pulled the bag to him. He then pushed it toward her. Leaning a hip against the cabinet as if he had no place he'd rather be, he asked, "So what happens now?"

"Are you asking for a play-by-play?" She spread flour across the counter.

"Maybe."

"I have to divide the dough." She pulled it apart

and set what she wasn't going to use right away back into the bowl.

"Why're you doing that?"

"This recipe makes two cakes. Are you sure there isn't a basketball game on that you want to watch?"

"Nope, I like watching you."

Focusing her attention on her baking again, she dumped the dough onto the granite corner top. She reached into one of the bags and pulled out a rolling pin.

"You didn't think I'd have one of those, did you?" Mark asked from his position beside her.

"Do you?"

"I'm sure I do around here somewhere. I'd have to hunt for it."

"That's why I brought my own." She punched the dough flat with her palms then picked up the pin and started rolling.

"While I roll this out, would you find the cinnamon? It's in one of these bags."

"Sure." He walked to the other side of the room and pulled a bowl out of the cabinet. They each did their jobs in silence."

Heat washed over her. She was far too aware

of him being near. All her disquiet went into making the dough thin and wide. "Would you also open the cream cheese? I set it out to soften earlier."

"Will do."

Laura Jo had never had a man help her in the kitchen. Her father had no interest in cooking, not even grilling. Phil had seen it as woman's work and never helped. It was nice to have someone interested in the same thing that she was. To work with her.

"I'm going to need the sugar. I forgot to bring any." Maybe if she kept him busy, he wouldn't stand so close.

"That I do have. Coming right up." Mark reached under the counter and pulled out a plastic container. "Here you go."

"Thanks." Laura Jo brushed her hair away with the back of her hand, sending flour dust into the air.

"Turn around," Mark said.

"Why?"

"Just turn around. For once just trust me."

Behind her there was the sound of a drawer being pulled open then pushed back.

"What are—?"

Mark stepped close enough that she felt his heat from her shoulders to her hips. Strong fingers glided over her scalp and fanned out, gathering her hair.

Her lungs began to hurt and she released the breath she held. Every part of her was aware of how close Mark stood. His body brushed hers as he moved to a different angle. One hand drifted over her temple to capture a stray strand. His warm breath fluttered across the nap of her neck. She quivered.

There was a tug then a pull before he said, "There, that should help."

He moved and the warmth that had had her heart racing disappeared, leaving her with a void that she feared only Mark could fill.

She touched the back of her head. He had tied her hair up with a rag. "Thanks."

"Now you can work without getting flour all in your hair."

He'd been doing something practical and she had been wound up about him being so close. She needed to finish these cakes and go home as soon as possible.

"Would you mind melting a stick of butter?"

"Not at all," Mark said in an all-too-cheerful manner.

Laura Jo continued to roll the dough into a rectangle, while keeping an eye on Mark as he moved around on the other side of the counter. "One more thing."

He raised a brow.

"Would you mix the cinnamon and sugar together?"

"Yeah. How much?" Mark headed again to where the bowls were.

"Like you are making cinnamon toast."

"How do you know I know how to make cinnamon toast?"

"Everyone knows how to do that," she said, as she finished rolling the first half of the dough. "While I roll out the other dough, will you spread butter on this one then put the sugar cinnamon mixture over that?"

"I don't know. All that might be out of my territory."

She chuckled. "I think you can handle it."

Over the next few minutes they each worked at their own projects. Laura Jo was used to making the cakes by herself but found she liked having a partner even in something as simple as a cake. She glanced at Mark. His full attention was on what he was doing. He approached his assignment much as he did giving medical care, with an effort to do the very best, not miss any detail.

She looked over to where he was meticulously shaking the sugar mixture on the dough from a spoon. "You know you really can't do that wrong."

"Uh?"

He must have been so involved in what he was doing he hadn't heard her. "Enjoy what you're doing a little. It doesn't have to be perfect."

Mark straightened. "This comes from the person who only laughs when my dog gets the best of me."

"I laugh at other times."

"Really?"

Was she truly that uptight? Maybe she was but she could tell that lately she'd been starting to ease up. Ever since she'd started spending time with Mark.

"Speaking of uptight, what's your issue with a wheelchair?"

CHAPTER FIVE

DAMN, SHE'D NOTICED. Mark had thought, hoped, Laura Jo had missed or he'd covered his feelings well enough when he'd seen a wheelchair, but apparently not.

Maybe he could bluff his way out of answering. "I don't know what you mean."

Laura Jo was looking at him. His skin tingled. He glanced at her. She had stopped what she was doing.

"Please, don't insult my intelligence," she said quietly.

He sighed before answering. "My friend who was in the accident is now in a wheelchair."

"I'm sorry to hear that."

"Me, too." He put the empty bowl in the sink.

"What happened?"

"He was thrown from the car."

"Oh, how awful."

"It was." He needed to change the subject. "So what do I need to do now?"

"Roll it into a log, like this." Laura Jo moved close and started working with the dough.

He looked at the honey nape of her neck exposed and waiting for him. Mike went out of his mind and all he could think about was the soft woman so close, the smell of cinnamon and sugar and the need to touch her, kiss her.

The wisps of hair at her neck fluttered as he leaned closer. He touched the tip of his tongue to her warm skin. He felt a tremor run through her and his manhood responded. His lips found the valley and he pressed. Sweet, so sweet.

She shifted away. "Mark, I don't have time in my life to play games."

"Who said I was playing a game?"

"I have Allie to think about."

He spoke from behind her. "So you're going to put how you feel and your life on hold for Allie? For how long?" He kissed her behind the ear.

Her hands stopped rolling the dough. She stepped to the side so that she could turn to look at him. "What I'm not going to do is get involved with a man I have no intention of marrying."

Mark put some space between them. "Whoa, we're not talking about marriage here. More like harmless fun. A few kisses. Some mutually satisfying petting." He stepped back and studied her. "Are you always this uptight around a man?"

"I'm not uptight."

"The best I can tell is the only time you're not is when I'm kissing you or you're laughing at my dog."

"I wasn't laughing at Gus. I was laughing at you."

He took a step closer, pinning her against the counter. "No one likes to be laughed at. But what I'm really interested in is you showing me how you're not uptight. I want to kiss you, Laura Jo. Just kiss you."

She didn't resist as his lips came down to meet hers. His mouth was firm but undemanding as if he was waiting to see if she would accept him. When had been the last time she had taken a moment's pleasure with a man? What would it hurt if she did? Just to have something that was simple and easy between two adults.

Laura Jo wrapped her hands around his neck, weaved her fingers through his hair and pressed herself against his lean, hard body. With a sigh, she returned his kiss.

Mark encircled her waist and lifted her against him. His mouth took further possession, sending wave after wave of heat through her. He ran the tip of his tongue along the seam of her mouth until she opened for him. The parry and thrust of his tongue had her joining him. He pressed her against the counter, shifted her until his desire stood ridged between them.

Something poked at her bottom just before there was a loud thump on the floor. She broke away. Mark's hand remained at her waist. Her breath was shallow and rapid. She was no longer a maiden but she sure was acting like one. Her heart was thudding against her rib cage. She couldn't look at Mark.

When she did glance at him through lowered lashes, to her great satisfaction he looked rattled, too. He leaned toward her again and she broke the embrace before stepping away. "I need to get these cakes ready to put in the oven." She was relieved that her voice sounded steadier than she felt.

Mark looked for a second as if he might disagree but he didn't move any closer.

"I think I like the sugar you just gave me better than what is on a king cake."

She had to regain her equilibrium. The only way she knew how to do that was to go on the defensive. She placed her hands on her hips. "You haven't tasted one of my cakes."

"No, but I have tasted you," he said in a soft and sultry voice.

Pleasure filled her. Mark had a way of making her feel special.

"Why don't you spread the cream cheese on this cake while I finish braiding the other one?"

"Yes, ma'am."

Minutes later Mark dropped the spatula he had been using in the sink. Laura Jo placed the cake she was working with on a baking pan. She had been aware of every movement he'd made as he'd spread the creamy cheese across the thin pastry.

"While you finish up on this one I'm going to get us each a bowl of gumbo." Mark went to a cabinet and pulled down two bowls.

Laura Jo was both relieved and disappointed when he moved to the other side of the center counter. If Mark was close he made her feel nervous and if he wasn't she missed his nearness.

"We forgot to put the babies in." Laura Jo reached into a bag and brought out a snack-size bag with tiny hard plastic babies in it. Their hands and feet were up in the air as if they were lying in a crib, laughing.

"I'll put those in. I promised Allie I would. I keep my promises."

Mark joined her again and she handed the babies to him. They looked extra-small in his large palm.

"Turn around. And don't peek."

Laura Jo did as he instructed.

"Okay. Done."

Laura Jo started cleaning up the area. "You know, it doesn't have to be such a secret. Mardi Gras will be over in four days and we won't be having another cake until next year."

He met her gaze. "Well, maybe I'll ask for something besides cake if I find the baby inside my piece."

"That's not how it works."

"Then we could just change the rules between us."

Laura Jo wasn't sure she wanted to play that game. "Are you ready for gumbo?"

"I can eat while these rise." She looked over at the cakes.

"I had no idea this much work went into making a king cake."

"They are labor intensive but I enjoy it. Especially when I can make them in a kitchen like this one."

Mark filled the two bowls he'd gotten out earlier. "Do you mind carrying your own bowl to the table?"

"Of course not. I don't expect you to wait on me."

They sat across from each other in the small breakfast nook adjoining the kitchen. From there they had a view of the bay.

"This is delicious." Laura Jo lifted a spoonful of gumbo. "I'm impressed with your culinary skills."

"I think culinary skills is a little strong. It's not hard really."

"Either way, it tastes good." She was glad that they were back to their old banter. She'd been afraid that after their hot kiss, which had her nerves on high alert, they wouldn't be able to have an easy conversation. She rather enjoyed their discussions, even if they didn't always agree.

"How's Marcy doing?"

She looked at him. "Very well, thanks to you. She'll be coming home tomorrow."

"I didn't do anything but provide encouragement. I meant to go by to see them again but I had to work late on the days I wasn't patrolling parades."

"Ann really appreciated the one day you did check in on them. That was nice of you."

"I'm a nice guy."

He really was. She'd done him a disservice when she'd first met him. He'd proven more than once that he was a good person.

"So have you found the funding for the shelter yet?" Mark asked as he pushed his empty bowl away.

"We qualified for the grant I was hoping for but it requires we find matching funds."

"Well, at least you do have some good news." He stood, gathering his bowl. "Do you want any more gumbo while I'm getting some?"

"No, I'm still working on this." Laura Jo watched him walk away. He wore a lightweight long-sleeved sweater and worn jeans. He really had a fine-looking butt.

For a second she'd been afraid he'd ask her about going to the dance. A hint of disappointment touched her when he didn't. He probably had a date with someone else by now. She didn't like that thought any better.

They finished their dinner with small talk about the weather, parades and the coming weekend. Together they carried their bowls to the dishwasher. Mark placed them in it while Laura Jo checked on the rising cake.

"How much longer on those?" Mark asked.

"They need to rise to double their size. Then I'll bake them and be on my way. I can finish the topping when I get home."

"Oh, no, you won't. I want to eat some as soon as you get them done. Besides, I want to do the topping."

"You're acting like Allie."

"Did you think I was kidding when I told you that I liked king cake as much as she did? I haven't had any in a long time and I'm not letting you out of the house without a piece today. While we're waiting, why don't we go out on the deck and have a cup of coffee and watch the sunset?"

She wasn't sure if watching the sunset with Mark was a good idea but she didn't know how to get out of it gracefully. Those darned cakes were taking too long to rise for her comfort. "Make that another glass of tea and I'll agree."

"Done. Why don't you go on out and take your pick of chairs and I'll bring the drinks."

Laura Jo walked through the living area and out one of the glass doors. Gus got up from his bed and ambled out with her. She took one of the lounges, making sure it wasn't near any others. Having Mark so close all the time was making her think of touching him, worse, kissing him again. She needed to put whatever distance she could between them.

Gus lay at the end of the lounge.

"Here you go," Mark said, placing her glass and his mug on the wire mesh table beside her. He then pulled one of the other lounges up on the opposite side of the table. He stretched his long body out and settled in.

"You mind handing me my mug?"

With shaking hands, Laura Jo passed him his drink.

"This is the best part of the day. I miss this when I have to work late."

She had to agree. It was nice to just slow down and be for a few minutes. "Is working here a lot different from your clinic in California?"

"The patients' backgrounds are different but sick people are sick people."

"Do you regret leaving California?"

"I have to admit I like the slower pace here." Mark crossed his ankles and settled more comfortably into the lounge.

"I couldn't leave Mobile and move all the way across the country."

"Sometimes you do things because you don't think you have a choice."

She watched a bird dipping into the water after its evening meal. "I know about not having choices." Maybe in some ways they weren't so different after all.

They both lapsed into silence as the sun slowly sank in the sky.

Laura Jo took a sip of her tea at the same time a breeze came in off the water. She shivered.

Mark put his mug down on the decking and stood. "I'll be back in a sec."

He returned with a jacket in his hand and handed it to her. "Here, you can put this on."

She slipped her arm into one sleeve and Mark held the jacket for her to put the other in. He sat beside her again. She trembled again and pulled the jacket closer around her.

As the wind blew, a scent of spice and musk that could only be Mark tickled her nostrils. She inhaled. For some reason it was a smell she wanted to remember.

Again they lapsed into a relaxed silence.

As the daylight was taken over by the night, Mark reached over and took her hand, weaving his fingers between hers. It was strong, secure and soothing. Laura Jo didn't pull away. Didn't want to.

When the stars came out Mark said, "We need to go and put those cakes in."

Laura Jo started. She'd been so content she'd forgotten about having anything to do. Her hand being surrounded by Mark's added to that feeling. For some reason it made her feel protected, as if she weren't facing the world alone. She hadn't had that in her life for so long it had taken her time to recognize it.

Mark not only made her feel protected but she had seen his security in tangible terms. He was great with Allie. More than once he'd seen to it that she was safe and cared for and that made her happy. She'd also seen him showing that protection to others. He'd been there when she'd called for help with Anna and Marcy. There hadn't been a moment's hesitation on his part about coming. Not once had he acted like her having a daughter was an issue. In fact, he embraced Allie, included her.

Why was Mark the one man who made her feel that way? His background said he wasn't the man for her. She wanted someone who was more interested in her than what her last name had been. But hadn't he proved her background didn't matter? He'd shown his interest well before she had told him her maiden name was Herron.

She might have questioned whether or not he had become a doctor for the money and prestige but the Clayborns already had that. After she'd viewed him seeing to a patient she'd seen his concern was sincere. He was a man interested

in caring for people. He had offered to help with
the shelter and had proved it with his donation
and medical care. How different could he be from
Phil, who was the most self-centered man she'd
ever known?

She slipped her hand out of his. "I'll bake
the cakes. You should stay here. It's a beautiful
night."

"I'll help you."

"It won't take me long."

"Do you promise to come back? Not disappear
out the front door?"

Laura Jo smiled. "Yes, I'll come back."

"I'll be waiting."

She liked the sound of that. People didn't wait
for her, they left her. Mark was starting to mean
too much to her. Laura Jo put the cakes in the
ovens. Thankfully, Mark had double ovens and
she could bake them at the same time.

Still wearing his jacket, she went back outside
to join him. If he hadn't stated his fear that she
might leave she might have considered going
home without telling him. Her attraction to him
was growing beyond her control. She didn't trust
herself around him.

As she passed him on the way to her lounge he sat up and snagged her wrist. "Come and sit with me." He pulled her toward him.

She put a hand down next to his thigh to stop herself from falling.

"Mark..." she cautioned.

"I'm not going to jump you. I'd just like to have you close."

"Why?"

The light from inside the house let her see well enough his incredulous look. "Why? Because I'm a man and you're a woman. I like you and I think you like me more than you want to admit. You're as aware of the attraction as I am. You just won't admit it.

She looked down at him for a moment.

"All I want is to sit here with a beautiful woman and watch the stars. Nothing more. But if you don't want to, I'll live with that."

He made it sound like she was acting childishly. "Scoot over."

"If you're going to get bossy then maybe I need to reconsider my invitation."

She snickered and lay on her side next to him.

He wrapped an arm around her shoulders and her head naturally went to his chest.

"Now, is this so bad?"

"No. I'm much warmer."

"Good. I'm glad I can be of service." Mark's breath brushed her temple.

"I can't get too comfortable. I don't want to burn the cakes."

"How much longer do they need to cook?" His hand moved up and down her arm.

"Another forty minutes."

He checked his watch. "Then I'll help you remember."

It took her a few minutes to relax and settle into her warm and cozy spot alongside Mark. The lights of Mobile glowed in the distance and the horn of an occasional seagoing freighter sounded. It was a lonesome noise, one that up until this minute she could identify with. Somehow she no longer felt lonely. As they sat in silence her eyelids drooped and closed.

The next thing she knew Mark was shaking her awake.

"We need to get the cakes out."

She jerked to a sitting position. "I'm sorry. I went to sleep on you."

"I'm not. It would be my guess you needed to rest after the week you've had."

Laura Jo couldn't argue with that. She struggled to get up.

"Let me climb out first then I'll pull you up," Mark suggested.

As he moved, his big body towered over her. She was tempted to touch him. Before she could stop herself she placed a hand on his chest.

"I'm squishing you?"

"No. I just wanted to touch you," she murmured.

He gave her a predatory glare. "Great. You decide to touch me when the king cakes might be burning. You need to work on your timing."

She nudged him back. "Let me up."

He hesitated a second before he took her hand and pulled her to her feet. "Let's go."

In the kitchen Mark peeked into an oven. He inhaled dramatically. "Smells wonderful."

"If you'll get your nose out of it, I can take it out." Laura Jo handed him a hot pad. "I'll get this one and you can get the other." Laura Jo pulled the golden-brown mound out of the oven and set it on the counter. Mark did the same and placed his beside hers.

Again he leaned over and inhaled deeply. "Perfect."

"I need to mix the icing and then we can put the colors on." Laura Jo found a bowl and added powdered sugar then water. She stirred them into a creamy white mixture. Using a spoon, she drizzled the icing back and forth over the top of the cakes.

Mark dipped a finger through the bowl and put it in his mouth. "Mmm."

She tapped the top of his hand when he started after the cake.

"Ouch."

"I believe you have a sweet tooth."

"I think you are sweet."

"I think you might flatter the cook in order to get your way. It's time for the colored sugar." Laura Jo picked up the food coloring she'd left on the other end of the counter. "We'll need three bowls."

Mark went to a cabinet and brought those to her. Laura Jo put granulated sugar in each of the bowls and added yellow coloring to one, purple to another and green to the last one. She mixed until each granule had turned the color. She sprinkled one color over a third of one cake. In the middle section another and on the last third another.

"Do you know what the colors stand for?" Mark asked.

"No self-respecting citizen of Mobile wouldn't know. Purple is for justice, green is for faith and gold for power."

"You are correct. Can we have a slice now?" Mark asked, sounding much like a child begging at his mother's side.

"You want to eat it while it's hot?"

"Why not?"

"I've just never had it that way. I've always waited until it's cooled."

"Well, there's a first time for everything." Mark pulled a knife out of a drawer and sliced a hunk off the end of one cake. Picking it up, he bit into it. "This is delicious. Allie is right, you do make the best cakes. I've never had one better from a bakery."

His praise made her feel warm inside. She cut

a small section and placed it in her mouth. It was good.

"Hey, look what I found." He held up a baby.

"You knew where that was."

"I did not," he said in an indignant tone. "Just good luck."

Laura smiled and placed the items she had brought into bags. She needed to leave before she was tempted to stay longer. Being with Mark had been far more enjoyable than she'd found comfortable. What if he tried to kiss her again? Could she handle that?

"What're you doing?" Mark asked.

"I'm packing up."

"You don't have to go."

"Yes, I do. Do you have something I can wrap one of these cakes in? Allie will be expecting to eat some tomorrow."

Mark opened a drawer and handed her a box of plastic wrap.

She pulled out a length of wrap and started covering the cake. "Do you mind if I take your baking pan? I'll return it."

"I don't mind," he said in an aggravated tone, as if he knew she was dodging the issue.

"Are you running out on me, Laura Jo?"

She refused to look at him. "No, I've been here for hours and I was more worried about wearing out my welcome."

Mark took the wrap from her and put it on the counter. "I don't think that's possible. I believe you're running scared."

"I'm not."

"Then why don't you go to the dance with me on Tuesday night?"

"I've already said I can't." She reached for a bag and put the rest of the items she'd brought in it.

"I think it's 'I won't.'"

"Please, Mark, just leave it alone. I'm not going to change my mind. It's not because of you but for other reasons."

"Care to tell me what those are."

"I'd rather not. I need to be going." She pulled the bags to her.

"I'm a good listener."

"That's not the problem. I just don't want to talk about it. Now, I need to go."

Mark took them from her. "I'll get these. You can get the cake. I'll walk you to your car."

Laura Jo was a little disappointed that he hadn't put up more of an argument to her leaving. Had her refusal to open up about why she didn't want to go to the krewe dance put him off? Wasn't that what she wanted?

"I need to wrap your cake up before I go and clean up this mess."

"Don't worry about doing that. I'll take care of it. Theresa will be in tomorrow."

"Theresa?"

"My housekeeper."

Just another shining example of the fact they lived in two different worlds. "Well, I'm not going to leave anyone, including a housekeeper, this mess."

"I'm not surprised. It's in your nature to see to other people, make it better for them. Who makes things better for you?"

She hadn't ever thought of herself in that context but he might be right. She wouldn't let him know it, though. "I don't need anyone taking care of me."

"We might be perfect for each other because I'm no good at doing so," he said in a dry tone.

What had made him say that? He was always taking care of people.

She went to the sink, picked up the cleaning cloth and started wiping off the counter.

"Leave it." Mark said, taking the cloth and placing it in the sink. "I'll take care of it."

Laura Jo then picked up the cake and headed for the front door. Mark wasn't far behind. When they reached the car, he opened the front passenger-side door and placed the bags on the floor. He then took the cake from her and did the same.

She went to the driver's door and he joined her there. "Thanks for helping me with the cakes."

"Not a problem." Mark reached into his pocket and pulled something out.

Laura Jo could just make out with the help of the light from the porch that he was rotating the baby between his index and thumb.

"We had a deal."

Laura Jo had an uneasy feeling. Where was he going with this? "We did."

"I would like to collect now."

Every nerve in her hummed. Something told her that she might not like his request. "Just what do you want?"

Mark's lips lifted, giving him a wolfish appearance. He took a step closer, coming into her personal space.

Heat washed over her. She looked at him. In the dim light she couldn't see his eyes clearly but she felt their intensity.

"I want you to kiss me."

"What?"

"I want you put your hands on my shoulders, lean up and place your lips on mine."

He said the words in a form of a challenge, as if she would refuse. She'd show him. Placing her hands on his chest, she slowly slid them up and over his shoulders.

His hands went to her waist, tightening around her.

"Remember this is my kiss," she admonished him.

He eased his hold but didn't release her.

Going up on her toes, she took her time, bringing her lips to his. The tension across his shoulders told her Mark was working to restrain himself.

Taking his lower lip between her teeth, she gently tugged.

He groaned.

She let go and smoothed it over with the tip of her tongue. Slowly she moved her lips over his until she almost ended the contact.

At Mark's sound of resistance she grinned and moved her mouth back to press it firmly against his. She didn't have to ask for entrance, he was already offering it. Her tongue met his and danced but he soon took the lead. She'd been caught at her own game. It felt wonderful to have a man touch her. It had been so long. For Mark to be the one made it even more amazing. Wrapping her arms around his neck, she gave herself over to the moment. She wanted more, so much more.

Mark gripped Laura Jo's waist and pulled her closer. He pressed her back against the car. His hand slid under the hem of her shirt and grazed her smooth skin until his fingers rested near the prize. Wanting to touch, taste, tease, he had to remove the barrier. Using the tip of his index finger, he followed the line of her bra around to the clasp. When he hesitated Laura Jo squirmed against him. She wanted this as much as he did.

Flicking the clasp open, he moved his hand to the side curve of her breast.

He released her lips and gave a small sound of complaint. Placing small kisses along her neck to reassure her, he skimmed his hand upward to cup her breast. His sigh of pleasure mingled with hers. He tested the weight. Perfect. Using a finger, he circled her nipple then tugged.

Her hips shifted and came into more intimate contact with his ridged manhood. He'd been aware of his desire for Laura Jo for a number of days but it had never been this overwhelming.

He pushed her bra up and off her other breast. Her nipple stood tall, waiting for his attention. That knowledge only fueled his desire.

Laura Jo cupped his face and brought his lips back to hers. She gave him the hottest kiss he'd ever received. Heaven help him, if she could turn him on with just kisses, what could she do to him in bed?

She ran her hands under his shirt and across his back.

When her mouth left his to kiss his cheek, he pushed up her shirt, exposing her breasts. He backed away just far enough to look at her. "Beautiful."

He didn't give her time to speak before his lips found hers again and his fingers caressed her breast. Thankful for her small car, he leaned her back over the hood. Her fingers flexed and released against the muscles of his back as she met him kiss for kiss. Standing between her legs, the heat of her center pressed against his. He pulled his mouth from hers. It went to the top of her right breast, where he placed his lips. Laura Jo shivered.

"Cold?"

"No."

His chest swelled with desire. What he was doing to her had caused the reaction, not the metal of the car. He lowered his mouth to her nipple and took it. Using his tongue, he spun and tugged. Laura Jo bucked beneath him.

Her hand went to the line of his pants and glided just beneath. She ran her hand one way and then the other before it returned to stroking his back.

She wasn't the cold fish she wanted him to believe she was. She was hot and all sensual woman. He smiled as he gave the other nipple the same devotion.

He wanted her here and now. In his driveway. On her car. But that wasn't what Laura Jo deserved. He wasn't that kind of man. She certainly wasn't that type of woman.

"Sweetheart, we need to go inside."

Mark saw her blink once, twice, as if she were coming out of a deep dream. She looked around as if trying to figure out where she was. He saw the moment she came back to reality and his heart dropped.

"Oh, God." She sat up and gave him a shove.

He stepped back and let her slide off the car.

She jerked her shirt down, not bothering to close her bra. "I have to go."

"No, you don't."

He stepped toward her and she stopped him with a hand. "I can't do this."

"Why not?"

"Because it is wrong for me on so many levels." She climbed behind the wheel of the car. "I'm sorry, Mark."

She couldn't have been any more sorry than he was. He stood there with his body as tight as a bike spoke, wanting to reach out to her. Laura Jo didn't even look at him as she started the car and headed out the drive.

It wasn't until the car stopped about halfway down that he knew she hadn't been as unaffected by what had passed between them as she'd acted. She had wanted him, too.

Guilt filled him. He had no business pursuing Laura Jo if he had no intention of the relationship going beyond what they had just experienced. He couldn't let it be more. He'd already proved he would run when the going got tough. Could he trust himself not to let them down, like he had Mike?

As her taillights disappeared, he turned and walked toward the house. All he had waiting for him tonight was a long, cold shower. He needed to stay well out of Laura Jo's life.

Laura Jo opened the door early the next morning to let Allie, Marsha and Jeremy in. Before Laura Jo could say hello, Marsha announced, "We've got a problem."

"Bigger than the one we already have?"

"Yep."

"Come on into the kitchen and tell me what's happened."

Marsha followed her while Jeremy rushed ahead and took the chair next to Allie.

Marsha sat in the other chair while Laura Jo got a bowl from the cabinet and placed it in front of Jeremy. She then sat down. "Okay, let me have it."

"I got an email from the city rep, saying that if we don't get half the asking price in cash to them by the end of next week then there's no deal,"

This was worse than Laura Jo had expected. "That only gives us five days, and three of those are holidays," she groaned.

"I know. That's why I'm here. Do you have any ideas?"

Laura Jo propped her elbows on the table and put her head in her hands. "No," she said in a mournful voice.

"I do," Marsha announced emphatically.

Laura Jo looked at her. "You do?"

"You have to go to the knewe dance. It's our only chance."

Laura Jo stood and walked to the sink. After last night, going to the dance had become less about her past and more about her reaction to Mark. She had been so tempted to throw all her responsibilities and concerns into the bay and find paradise in his arms. She'd been lying half-naked on the hood of a car, for heaven's sake. The man made her lose her mind. She'd had to stop at the end of his drive in order to get herself together enough to drive. Her hands had still been shaking when she'd started across the bay.

She couldn't stand the thought of losing the best chance they'd had in years to have a new house. But if she went to the dance she'd have to resist Mark, which she wasn't sure she could do, and face her parents and the social circle she'd left behind. The one she spoke so negatively about. She would be going back with her tail between her legs and begging them to help her. No, she would be asking for help for the shelter. It had nothing to do with her personally.

"I'll call Mark. If he hasn't asked someone else to go, I'll tell him I'll go."

Marsha joined her at the sink. "I wouldn't ask you to do it if I thought there was another way." She put an arm around Laura Jo's shoulders. "The house is too perfect for us not to give it our best shot. I'd go but I don't have the same influence as you or Dr. Clayborn have."

"I know. I just hope it works." Maybe going would not only benefit the house but give her a chance to lay some ghosts to rest.

"Me, too." Marsha squeezed her shoulder.

What if Mark had already found another date? That thought gave Laura Jo a sick feeling. Then she guessed she'd be going to the dance by herself. Not only to face her past alone but to see Mark holding another woman. Neither experience appealed to her.

CHAPTER SIX

IT WAS MIDMORNING and Mark was at his office desk when the woman he'd been planning to ask to the dance informed him that he had a call.

Picking up the phone, he said, "Dr. Clayborn here."

"Mark, its Laura Jo."

Like he wouldn't recognize her voice.

"If you don't already have a date for the dance, I'd like to go after all," she finished on a breathless note.

He'd thought of little else but her since those minutes outside his home. She'd kissed him so thoroughly, leaving him in need of not only one cold shower but two. Laura Jo had completely turned the tables on him with those hot, sexy kisses. He'd only hoped to kiss her one more time but instead he'd been left wanting all of her.

"No, I haven't asked anyone else yet."

After the way she'd left last night, something

bad must have happened regarding the shelter for her to agree to go to the dance with him. He didn't care, he wasn't going to question the gift.

"So I'm still invited?"

"If you would like to go."

"I would."

"So what changed your mind?"

"They've moved up the timetable on the shelter house and I've been left no choice."

"Well, it's nice to know it isn't because you might enjoy an evening out with me," he said in his best serious tone.

He had to admit it stung to know that she had no interest in being seen at the most prestigious event of the year with him. The only reason she had agreed to go was because she needed help finding funds for the shelter. She had made it clear on more than one occasion that she didn't want to go, so he could only imagine how desperate she must be to pick up the phone and call him. She wanted that shelter enough to take this bold step. What impressed him most was that it wasn't for her but for someone else.

"I'll pick you up at seven."

"Make it eight. I have to work the parade."

That figured. When did she ever take time for herself? He was going to see to it that she enjoyed the evening out with him if it killed him.

"I'll be there at eight, then. We'll make a grand entrance."

"That's what I'm afraid of. Bye, Mark." With that she rang off.

"Laura Jo, stop fussing, you look beautiful," Marsha nagged as Laura Jo pulled up on the dress that showed far too much cleavage for her comfort.

She'd found the evening dress at the upscale consignment shop downtown. Ironically, it was the same one her mother had taken all the family's outdated clothes to when Laura Jo had been a child. Her mother would say, "Maybe someone less fortunate can use these." Like people who were less fortunate cared whether or not they wore couture clothing.

"I'm only going to this thing to try to drum up funds for the shelter, not to have men staring at me. I'll have to wear the green dress. Would you get it? It's in my closet."

Laura Jo hadn't had time to look any further

for a more appropriate dress. She'd taken the first one that was her size and looked suitable. She hadn't even tried it on and had had no idea this one would be so revealing.

"Isn't the dress formal?" Marsha said, as if she were reassuring a child having a temper tantrum.

"Yes, but I guess I don't have a choice." Laura Jo looked into the full-length mirror one more time. The plunging neckline left the top of her breasts exposed. Each time she breathed she feared more than that might be visible. For a brief second the memory of Mark's lips pressed against her flesh made her sizzle all over. She inhaled sharply.

"Is something wrong?" Marsha asked.

She circled around and faced Marsha. "Don't you have a pink shawl? I could put it around my shoulders and tie it in front. That would fix the problem."

Marsha sighed. "I don't see a problem but I'll go get it. I think you're overreacting. The dress is perfect the way it is."

Laura Jo looked at herself again. Was she over-reacting? If so, why? Because she was going to the dance with Mark or because she was afraid she couldn't control herself around him?

She studied the dress. It was midnight blue with the slightest shimmer to it. The material hugged her in all the correct places. Twisting, she turned so that she could see the back. It closed close to her neck so that it formed a diamond-shaped peephole in the middle. It was the loveliest detail of the dress.

"Mommy, you look pretty," Allie said from behind Laura Jo.

"Thank you, honey." She leaned down and kissed the top of Allie's head.

The doorbell rang.

"I'll get it," Allie said, running out of the room.

Laura Jo followed. Surely it was Marsha, returning with the wrap.

Allie opened the door and Mark stood on the other side. Their eyes met and held. Everything that had happened between them the night before flashed through her mind. His gaze slid downward and paused at her breasts.

They tingled and her nipples grew hard. Heat pooled in her middle. What was happening to her? Something as simple as a look from Mark could make her feel alive like no one else could.

Was he remembering, too?

"Doesn't Mommy look pretty?" Allie asked, looking back and forth between them.

Mark's gaze didn't leave her. Seconds later, as if coming out of a stupor, he said, "Uh, yes, she looks wonderful."

Laura Jo swallowed hard. She'd never felt more beautiful than she did right now as Mark admired her. The man was starting to get under her skin and everything about his idea of life was so wrong for her. Or was it? She'd better guard her heart tonight or he might take it.

Allie looked up at Mark. "You look pretty, too."

He did, in the most handsome, debonair and charming way. His blond waves were in place and his eyes shone. Dressed in his formal wear of starched white shirt, black studs and tailcoat, he took her breath away. She'd seen many men wearing their finest but none compared to the man standing before her.

"Thank you, Allie." He was still looking at her when he said, "Do you mind if I come in?"

"Oh, no, do." Laura Jo gave Allie a little nudge

back into the hall. She stepped out of the way and let Mark enter.

"Come in and have a seat. I'm waiting for Marsha to bring me a cover-up."

"From where I stand, you look perfect just the way you are." His voice had a grainy sound to it that wasn't normal.

"Thank you." When had she become such a blusher? When Mark had come into her life.

"Have a seat while I get my purse. Marsha should be back by then." Laura Jo indicated a chair in their small living area.

There was a knock on the door and Allie ran to open it. Laura Jo trailed behind her. Her friend breezed in, breathless. "I couldn't find it. I must have given it away at our last clothes drive. Hi, Dr. Clayborn. You look nice." Marsha let the last few words spin out.

"Thank you. I was telling Laura Jo she looks great just as she is."

"I think so, too." Marsha said. She offered a hand to Allie. "Come on. It's time to go. Jeremy will be home in a few minutes."

Laura Jo picked up a small bag and handed it to her daughter. "I'll see you tomorrow afternoon.

I'll be picking you and Jeremy up from school." Laura Jo kissed her on the head.

"Okay. Bye, Mark." Allie happily went out the door.

"Have a good time and don't do anything I wouldn't do," Marsha quipped with a wink.

"Marsha!"

Mark's low chuckle didn't help to lessen Laura Jo's mortification.

She turned to him. "You do understand I'm only going to the krewe dance because I need funds for the shelter. Nothing else can happen."

"You more than made it clear that the evening has nothing to do with my company. Are you ready?"

Had she hurt his feelings?

"Mark, I'm sorry. I didn't mean to sound so rude." She looked down. "After the other night I just didn't want you to get the wrong idea. I do appreciate you taking me to the dance. It's just that I have a difficult time with the idea and I seem to be taking it out on you."

"Maybe if you explained, I would understand."

She looked at him again. "It's because...I shunned that world years ago."

"Why?"

"I fell in love, or at least what I thought was love, with a guy who my parents didn't approve of. 'Not of our social status,' my father said. My parents were adamantly against the marriage. They told me Phil was after my name and money, not me. That he was no good. My father was particularly vocal about Phil being the wrong guy. He forced me to make a choice between them or my ex.

"I always felt like I was an afterthought to them. I never quite fit the mold they had imagined for their child. They spent little time with me when I was young and now they wanted to start making parental demands, showing real interest. I had always been more headstrong than they liked, so my father's ultimatum backfired.

"I told my parents if the man I loved wasn't good enough for them then I didn't need them. I chose Phil. Turned out they were right about him. He was everything they said he was and more. I said some ugly things to my parents that I now regret but I couldn't go running back. My pride wouldn't allow that. I had to prove to them and myself I could take care of myself. Live with my mistakes."

Laura Jo would never let Mark know what it took for her to admit her mistakes. No matter how many times or how sweetly Marsha had asked Laura Jo, she had never told her as much as she had just told Mark.

"You haven't spoken to your parents in all that time?"

"I tried to contact them after Phil and I got back from Vegas but the housekeeper told me Mother wouldn't take my call. I phoned a few more times and got the same response. I finally gave up."

"They really hurt you."

Laura Jo fingered a fold in her dress. "Yes. After I had Allie I had a better sense of what it was to have a child's best interests at heart. But after they'd acted the way they did when I called I couldn't take the chance that they would treat Allie the same way as they had me. I'll never let her feel unwanted."

"Maybe they've changed. They might be better grandparents than they were parents. You could try again. At least let them meet Allie."

She shook her head. "I think the hurt is too deep and has gone on for too long."

"You'll never know until you try. I could go with you, if you want."

"I don't know. I'll have to think about that. Let's just get through tonight, then I'll see."

"I'll be there beside you all night. We'll both put in the appearance to get what you need and to also satisfy my father. Then we're out of there."

To her surprise, he didn't sound like he'd been that excited about going to the dance to begin with. Had she made some judgment calls about him that just weren't true? He'd never once looked down on her, her friends or where she lived. Did his status in the area truly not matter to him?

She made a chuckling sound that had nothing to do with humor and more about being resigned. "We sound nothing like two people expecting to enjoy an evening out."

At the car, he opened the door, took her elbow and helped her in. At least if she had to go to the dance she would arrive in a fine car and on the arm of the most handsome man in town.

Mark settled behind the wheel and closed the door but didn't start the engine. Instead, he placed his hand over hers. Squeezing it gently, he said, "I can see by the look on your face that you have no hope of this evening ending well. Why don't you think positive? You might be surprised."

"I'll try."

"Plus you're starting to damage my ego by making me think I no longer know how to show a woman a good time." Mark started the car then checked to see if she was buckled in. She patted her seat belt and he backed out of the parking space.

"This doesn't have anything to do with you personally." She studied his strong profile in the dim light.

"Well, I'm glad to know that. I was starting to think you thought being seen with me was comparable to going to the gallows."

She smiled.

"That's better. At least you haven't lost your sense of humor completely." He pulled out into the street.

They rode down now crowd-free Government Street toward the port. The building where the dance was being held was located on the bay.

Mark circled to the elegant glass doors of the historic building.

Mark stopped the car. He handed the keys to the valet then came around to open the door for her. Taking a deep fortifying breath, she placed her hand into Mark's offered one. It was large and steady.

"You're an outstanding nurse, mother of a wonderful daughter and an advocate for mothers, Laura Jo. You're more accomplished than the majority of the people here."

She met his look. His eyes didn't waver. He'd said what he believed. She drew confidence from that. "Thank you."

He pulled her hand into the crook of his arm as they walked toward the door of the building held open by another young man in evening dress. Slowly they ascended one side of the U-shaped staircase to the large room above. Mark paused at the door just long enough for her to survey the space.

People were standing in groups, talking. The room was narrow and long with a black-and-white-tiled floor. Round dining tables were arranged to the right and left, creating an aisle down the middle. The white tablecloths brushed the floor. The Mardi Gras colored decorations centered on each table were elaborate and striking.

The area looked much as it had the last time she'd attended a ball when she'd been nineteen years old and a lady-in-waiting. A month later she'd met Phil and her world had taken a one-eighty-degree turn. Back then she'd been a child of wealthy parents with her life planned out for her. When she'd broken away from her parents, she would never have guessed her life would become what it was now. Still, had she made a mistake by keeping Allie away from them? Her parents had faults but didn't she, too?

Just as eye-catching was the dress of the active men of the krewe. They were all clad in their Louis XVI brocade knee-length satin coats trimmed in gold or silver braid. On their heads were large hats that had one side of the brim pinned up with a plumed feather attached and matched the men's coats. Their pantaloons, white stockings and black buckle shoes added to the mystique. The women who were married to the members of the board wore equally ostentatious dresses, some of them matching their husband's. Otherwise, men and women were dressed in formal wear.

Were her parents here in all their finery?

Mark must have felt her stiffen because he placed his hand over hers, which was resting on his arm. "Let's go see and be seen."

They hadn't walked far when they were stopped by a man's voice calling, "Mark Clayborn, I heard you were back in town."

Mark brought her around with him. "Mr. Washington, how in the world are you?" Mark shook the man's hand and Laura Jo released his arm but remained beside him.

"I'm doing well."

"I heard about your father. He's recovering, I understand," the older man said.

"Slowly, but retirement is a must," Mark told Mr. Washington with ease.

"I imagine that's difficult for him. I'll make plans to get out to see him."

"I know he would like that."

When she started to move away Mark rested a hand at her waist. It warmed her skin. She was no longer worried about the people they might see. Her focus was on his touch.

Mr. Washington turned his gaze to her. Laura Jo knew who he was but had never met him.

Mark followed his look. "Mr. Washington, I'd like to introduce you to Laura Jo Akins."

Would he recognize her name? No, probably not. There were a number of girls in the south with double first names. Laura Jo wasn't that uncommon.

"Nice to meet you, Ms. Akins."

She forced a smile. "Nice to meet you, too." At least with her married name it wasn't obvious who she was.

"Laura Jo is a nurse at Mobile General and has started a shelter for abandoned mothers." Mark jumped right into helping her look for supporters.

"That sounds like a worthy cause," Mr. Washington said, as if he was really interested. "What made you decide to do that?"

Laura Jo wasn't going to lie. "I was an abandoned mother. My husband left me when I was pregnant. I have a daughter."

"So you know the need firsthand." He nodded his head thoughtfully.

"I do." Laura Jo lapsed into her planned appeal. Mark offered a few comments and the fact he had made a donation to what he thought was a worthy cause.

"Contact my office tomorrow and I'll have a donation for you," Mr. Washington assured her.

"Thank you. The women I'm helping thank you also."

Mark looked across the room. "Mr. Washington, I think it's time for us to find a place at a table for dinner."

"It does look that way. Good to see you, son. Nice to meet you, young lady."

As Mark led her away she whispered to him, "I never imagined it would be that easy."

"I don't think it will always happen that way. But Mardi Gras season is when people are having fun so they're a little more generous." He took her hand and led her farther into the room.

"You're right about coming tonight. As much as I didn't want to, it was the right thing to do for the shelter."

After they were stopped a couple of times by people Mark knew, he found them a table with two seats left near the front of the room. She still hadn't seen her parents.

Mark remained a gentleman and pulled her chair out for her before he took his own. She could get used to this. As ugly as she had been about coming to the ball, he'd still helped her get a promise of funds from Mr. Washington and was treating her like a lady. She owed him an apology.

He knew a few people sharing their table and introduced her. She recognized a number of other couples by their names but they didn't act as if they knew her. Still, she might run into some of her parents' friends. She looked around.

Mark whispered in her ear, "They might not be here."

Laura Jo knew better. They didn't miss a Mardi Gras ball. One more pass over the crowd and she saw them. They had aged well. There was more gray hair at her father's temples but her mother had a stylish cut and kept it colored. They both looked as elegant as they ever had for one of these events.

"What's wrong?"

"My parents."

Mark looked in the direction she indicated. "Why don't we go and say hello?"

"They won't want to speak to me. I said some horrible things to them."

"I bet that doesn't matter anymore. At least you could give them a chance. They may regret what happened, just like you do. You'll feel better if you do. At least you will know you made the effort. Come on, I'll be right there with you." He stood and offered his hand.

Laura Jo hesitated then placed her hand in Mark's. It was large, warm and strong. A new resolve filled her. No longer the same person she had been nine years ago, she could do this. Mark held her hand tight as they crossed the room. The closer they came to her parents' table the more her gut tightened. The sudden need to run splashed over her. She hesitated.

"You can do this." The small squeeze of her hand told her she wasn't alone.

Her parents looked up at them. Shock registered on their faces.

Mark let go of her hand and cupped her elbow.

"Hello, Mother and Daddy."

"We're surprised to see you here. We had no

idea you were coming," her father said in a blunt, boardroom voice.

Well, he was certainly all open arms about seeing her again.

"Hello, I'm Mark Clayborn. Nice to meet you, Mr. and Mrs. Herron."

Her parents looked at Mark as if they weren't sure they had heard correctly. She was just relieved he'd taken the attention off her for a moment.

"Mark Clayborn, junior?" her father asked.

"Yes, sir."

Her father stood and offered his hand. "Pleasure to meet you."

Leaving her seat, her mother came to stand beside her father. "How have you been, Laura Jo?"

She sounded as if she truly cared. "Fine."

"I'm glad to hear that. I understand you've started some type of shelter."

How did they know about that? Was she really interested? "I have."

Mark put an arm around her shoulders. "Laura Jo has helped a lot of women who needed it."

It was nice to have someone sound proud of

her. Not till this moment had she realized she'd been missing that in her life.

"Are they unwed mothers?"

At least her mother had asked with what sounded like sincere curiosity. "Some are but most have been abandoned. Those that have no family they can or want to go home to."

Laura Jo didn't miss her mother's flinch.

"That sounds like a worthwhile project," her mother finally said.

"It is," Mark agreed. "She's now trying to buy a larger place for the shelter to move to."

Laura Jo placed her hand on Mark's arm. She didn't want to go into all that with her parents. "I don't think they want to hear all about that."

When Mark started to argue she added, "How have you both been?"

"We've been well," her father said.

They were talking to each other like strangers, which in reality they were.

"I understand you live over in the Calen area."

"I do." Laura Jo was astonished that he knew that. Had they been keeping up with her when she'd had no idea? Did her parents care more than she'd thought or shown?

Her mother stepped toward Laura Jo with an imploring look on her face. "Will you tell us about our granddaughter?"

"You knew?" Laura Jo was thankful for Mark's steady hand steady on her elbow.

"Yes, we've known for a long time." Her mother's look didn't waver.

They had known and they still hadn't helped? Or they'd known that Laura Jo would throw their help back at them if they offered?

"Please, tell us about her," her father pleaded.

Laura Jo spent the next few minutes telling her parents about Allie. They seemed to hang on every word. Had they changed?

"Thank you for telling us," her mother said with a soft sigh when Laura Jo finished.

They were interrupted by the krewe captain getting the attention of the people in the room. He announced the buffet dinner was being served and gave directions about which tables would go first.

"We should return to our table," Laura Jo said.

It was her mother's turn to give her an entreating look. "Laura Jo, may we see Allie sometime?"

Laura Jo stiffened but she forced her voice to remain even. "I'll have to think about that. She knows nothing about you."

Moisture spring to her mother's eyes.

The table next to her parents' rose to get in line for their meal.

"I think it's time that we returned to our table, Laura Jo. It was nice to meet you both, Mr. and Mrs. Herron."

Mr. Herron blinked as if he had forgotten Mark was standing there.

"Thank you for coming over, Laura Jo. It's wonderful to see you."

Her mother sounded like she truly meant it.

"It's nice to see you, too." Laura Jo turned and headed back to their table on shaky knees.

Mark leaned in and asked, "You okay?"

"I'm good." She smiled. "Really good, actually. Thanks for encouraging me to speak to them."

He grinned. "Hey, that's what a good date does. So are you going to introduce Allie to them?"

"I don't know if I'm ready for that but at least I'll think about it."

"Sounds like a plan. Hungry?"

"Much more than I was a few minutes ago."

"Good."

They returned to their table and had to wait until a few tables on the other side of the room lined up and then it was their turn. Mark placed his hand at the small of her back again. As disconcerting as it was to have him touch her, he'd done it enough over the past couple of weeks that she'd grown to not only expect it but to appreciate the simple gesture.

They were almost to the buffet tables in the middle of the room when Mark jerked to a stop. She turned to question him about what was wrong. He stood looking in the direction of a group of people who were obviously together. His face had darkened. All pleasantness of a few minutes ago had washed away. One of the group was in a wheelchair. Did he know the man?

Mark quickly regained his composure and closed the gap between him and her.

"Are you okay?" she whispered when he came to stand next to her.

"I'm fine." He added a smile that for once didn't reach his eyes.

They stood in line for a few minutes, working their way to where the plates were stacked. A large floral arrangement was positioned where the tables intersected. On the four tables were shrimp cocktail, gumbo, salads of all types and prime rib, with a man serving that and desserts.

As they slowly filled their plates, Laura Jo saw Mark glancing toward the end of the line. She noticed the man in the wheelchair. This time Mark seemed even more uncomfortable about the situation.

As they went through the line Mark spoke to people. Thankfully everyone accepted her as his date and nothing more. Maybe she could get through this evening after all. She'd been a teenager when she'd last been at this kind of function. She had matured and changed since then.

During the meal, Mark spoke to the woman to the right of him. Laura Jo had a light conversation with the man in full regalia to her left. Once during the meal Mark gave her knee a reassuring squeeze. That little gesture said, We're in this together. She appreciated it. Except for Marsha, it had been her and Allie against the world.

She had finished her dinner when Mark got her attention and asked her to tell the woman he'd been talking to about the shelter. The woman told

Laura Jo that she would like to help and how to contact her.

The conversation was interrupted by the captain announcing that it was time to introduce the krewe directors.

Laura Jo smiled at Mark and mouthed, "Thank you."

He put his arm around her shoulder and gave her a gentle hug and whispered in her ear, "You're welcome. See, it's not as bad as you thought."

"No, it hasn't been. Thanks to you."

He kissed her temple. "You can really thank me later."

Before she could react to that statement the captain started calling names and people were lining up on the dance floor that was acting as a stage.

It was her turn to feel Mark stiffen. She saw the man in the wheelchair Mark had looked at earlier propelling himself across the stage, while an attractive woman walked beside him.

She glanced at Mark. His focus was fixed on the man. "Do you know him?"

"Yes."

"He's your friend from the accident, isn't he?"

"Yes." The word had a remorseful note to it.

The next man was being introduced and she didn't ask Mark any more. With everyone having been presented, the crowd clapped in appreciation for the work the board had done on the dance.

The captain then asked for everyone's attention again. "The king and queen and their court have arrived."

There was a hush over the room as the first lady-in-waiting and her escort were introduced.

The young lady wore an all-white dress made out of satin and adorned with pearls and sparkling stones. Her white train trailed across the floor. It was heavy, Laura Jo knew from experience.

When she had designed her train so many years ago it had had the family crest in the center with a large, pale pink flamingo rising from it. The bird's eye had been an onyx from her grandmother's train when she had been queen. Each pearl and precious stone were sewn on by hand. It had been edged in real white fox fur. She'd worn long white gloves that had reached above her elbows. She'd been told she'd never looked more beautiful.

And this happened every year. The pomp and circumstance of it all still astounded her.

She and her mother had designed and planned her dress and train for months. They had even taken a trip to New York to look for material. A designer there had made the dress then it had been sent back to Mobile, where a seamstress that specialized in embellishments had added them. What she would wear consumed their family life for the entire year before Mardi Gras.

She had no idea what her dress and train had cost but she was sure it would have been enough to run the shelter for two or three months.

"I bet you were a beautiful lady-in-waiting. I'm sorry I didn't pay more attention," Mark whispered close to her ear.

She smiled.

The couple walked to the captain and his wife on the stage and curtsied and bowed, before circling back to the rear of the room. By that time another couple had moved forward. The entire court was dressed in white, with the females having different dress and trains that had their personal design. The escorts wore identical outfits.

Each couple paid their respects and this happened eighteen more times.

From the court would come next year's king and queen of Mardi Gras. Since her grandmother had been queen, Laura Jo had been on track to be the queen the year she turned twenty-one. The king would reign the year he turned twenty-five.

She glanced at Mark, who was watching the stage more than the couples parading up the aisle. "I did notice you and you were a handsome king," Laura Jo whispered.

"Thank you, fair maiden."

Laura Jo giggled. She knew well that there was a private and public side to Mardi Gras. It all started around Thanksgiving, with all the coming-out balls for the girls. The society families held the balls and she'd been a part of the process. She'd loved it at the time. Now she looked back on it and saw how spoiled she been and how ignorant of the world. Not until she had gotten away from her parents' house had she realized how many people could have been helped with the money that had gone into just her dresses for Mardi Gras.

As the royalty came into sight, Laura Jo couldn't

help but be amazed at the beauty of the couple's attire. No matter how many times she had seen this type of event, she was still left in awe. They wore matching gold outfits trimmed in gold. The king's clothing was adorned as much as the queen's. She had gold beads that came to a peak halfway up the center of her skirt. The bodice had swirls and curls covering it. They carried crowns on their heads that glittered in the lights. The king carried a diamond-headed walking stick while the queen held a scepter that matched her crown.

Laura Jo had forgotten the artistry and how regal their trains were. They were both at least twenty feet long. Theirs, like those of the ladies-in-waiting, told a story of their life. The king's had his family crest with a hunting motif around it, which included an appliqué of a deer head. The queen's train was also appliquéd but with large magnolias in detail. Around the edge was a five-inch border of crystals that made it shimmer. The neckline had a collar that went from one shoulder to the other in the back. It stood up eight inches high. It bounced gently as the queen walked. It was made from a mass of light and airy bangle beads formed into magnolias and leaves, the centers being made out of pearls.

Their trains alone could buy a room in the house they were looking at for the shelter.

"How did it feel to be the man of the hour?" Laura Jo asked Mark.

"At the time, amazing," he answered in a dry tone.

CHAPTER SEVEN

WITH THE INTRODUCTIONS COMPLETED, everyone returned to their meals and the band struck up a dance tune. Couples moved toward the dance floor.

"Why don't we have a dance before we go and talk to a few more people about the shelter? I think we could both use a few minutes of fun." Mark stood and offered her his hand.

"One dance."

As they entered the dance floor he brought Laura Jo close. She fit perfectly. Wearing high heels, her head came to his shoulder. The band was just beginning the first notes of a slow waltz. Laura Jo put her hand in his and the other on his shoulder. His hand rested on the warm, creamy skin visible on her back.

"You know, I think I like this dress more now than I did when I first saw you in it." The words were for her alone.

She glanced up, giving him a shy smile. See-ing her parents again seemed to have taken some fight out of her. She had to have missed them more than she'd admitted. Leaning in, she put her head into the curve of his shoulder. Mark tight-ened his hold and slowly moved them around the dance floor.

Other couples surrounded them but for him there was only he and Laura Jo. For once he wished he could hold one woman forever. He'd never allowed himself to dream further but with Laura Jo anything seemed possible.

They were returning to their table when Mr. Washington approached. "I was telling a buddy of mine about the work your young lady is doing. He would like to pledge fifty thousand."

Laura Jo gasped.

"Baba McClure has had a little too much to drink already and he has pledged another fifty."

Laura Jo squeezed his arm.

"The thing is," Mr. Washington went on, "you'd better go over there and get something in writ-ing or they may not remember in the morning."

"Do you have a paper and pen in your purse?" Mark asked Laura Jo.

She picked up the tiny purse she had brought. "I have a small pen. I'll ask at the registration table if they have something we can write on."

Mark watched Laura Jo go. She was soon back. Mr. Washington showed them across the room and introduced them to the two men and let Laura Jo take it from there. Despite wanting to distance herself from her background, she had a way of charming people that had been instilled in her. She soon had a makeshift agreement from both men and had promised she would see them the next day.

Both men groaned and asked her to make it the day after. Before they left the table she gave Mr. Washington a kiss on the cheek. "Thank you."

The eighty-year-old man beamed. "You're welcome, honey."

"Come on, I believe this deserves a victory dance." She pulled Mark to the dance floor. A fast tune was being played.

"I don't fast-dance." Mark pulled to a stop.

"What was it you told me? Uh…let go a little." Laura Jo started moving to the music. She held her hands out, encouraging him to take them.

He wasn't going to turn that invitation down.

After a few dances, both fast and slow, he said, "I'm ready to go if you are."

"You're really not any more into this stuff than I am, are you?"

"No, I guess being in California for so long got it out of my system." And what had happened to Mike.

He had glimpsed Mike a couple of times across the room. They had never been near each other and for that Mark was grateful. Once he had thought his onetime friend might have recognized him. Dodging Mike didn't make Mark feel any better. He still couldn't face him. He used having Laura Jo with him as an excuse not to.

"Let's go," Laura Jo agreed. "But I need to stop by the restroom on our way out."

Mark was waiting at the exit when Mike rolled up.

"So was the plan to leave without speaking to me?" he asked, looking directly at Mark. "Running out again?"

He stood dumbstruck. His gut churned. If Laura Jo showed up, would she recognize what a coward he was?

"No," Mark lied boldly. If he could figure out

how to leave without having this conversation, he would. "I hadn't realized you were here." Another lie. "It's good to see you." At least that had a small margin of truth.

"I'm not sure that's true." Mike's gaze hadn't wavered.

The ache in Mark's chest increased.

"I hear you're back in town and practicing medicine."

"Yes, I'm in a clinic in Spanish Fort and living in Fairhope." If he could just make it through some small talk, Laura Jo would show up and they could go.

"You always did like it at the summer house," Mike said.

Mark glanced toward the other side of the room. "How have you been? I'm sorry I haven't—"

A blonde woman with twinkling green eyes and a cheery smile approached. "I'd like you to meet my wife." He reached behind him and took the hand of the woman. "This is Tammy."

Mike married? "It's nice to meet you."

"And you, too. Mike has told me a lot about you." Tammy continued to smile but it no longer reached her eyes.

Like how he'd been the cause of Mike being in a wheelchair for life, or the fact he had run out on him when he'd needed him most, or maybe the part where he hadn't bothered to stay in touch, like he should have. Yeah, there was a lot to say about him, but none of it good. Or to be proud of.

Laura Jo walked up beside him. Could she see how uncomfortable he was? He took her hand and drew her forward. "Uh, this is my friend Laura Jo. Laura Jo, Mike and Tammy Egan."

"Hey, I remember a Laura Jo. She was a friend of my kid sister's. I haven't seen her in years." Mike gave her a searching look.

"You're Megan's brother?" Laura Jo studied Mike for a moment.

Great. Mike remembered Laura Jo when he himself hadn't. He truly had been a self-absorbed person in his twenties. Maybe in many ways he still was.

"Yes, and you're Laura Jo Herron."

She smiled at Mike. "Was Herron. Now it's Akins."

"No matter the name, it's good to see you again."

It was time to get out of there. Mark said,

"Mike, I'm sorry, we're expected at another dance." Great. He was still running from Mike and lying to do so.

Laura Jo glanced at him but said nothing.

Mike rolled back and forth in his chair with the ease and agility of someone who had mastered the wheelchair. "I understand."

Somehow Mark was sure he did. All he wanted was to get away, forget, and find some fresh air. "Nice to see you again, Mike." Mark headed for the door. It wasn't until Laura Jo put her hand in his that he realized he had forgotten about her. He was running blind.

Mark didn't say anything on the way to his house. Laura Jo didn't either. They had both had an emotional evening. She let him remain in his thoughts, not even interrupting him to mention that he wasn't going toward her apartment. He didn't even register that he'd driven to his house until he'd pulled to a stop in his drive. "Why didn't you tell me to take you home?"

"Because I thought you needed someone to talk to."

How like her to recognize when someone was

having trouble. He was in need, but of all the people he didn't want to look weak in front of it was Laura Jo.

"Let's go in. I'll fix us a cup of coffee." She was already in the process of opening the car door. Inside the house, she dropped her purse on the table beside the door, kicked off her shoes then headed straight for the kitchen. When he started to follow she said, "Why don't you go out to the deck? I'll bring it to you."

"Thanks. I appreciate it." He sounded weary even to his own ears.

"I'm just repaying all the times you've been there for me."

On the deck he sat in one of the chairs, spread his knees wide and braced his elbows on them. Putting his head in his hands, he closed his eyes.

Seeing Mike tonight had been as tough as it had ever been. Mark had prepared himself that he might see him at the dance but that didn't make it any easier. It only added another bag of guilt to the ten thousand he already carried on his shoulders.

Now, with Laura Jo having seen his shame, it made the situation worse.

"Here you go," she said from beside him.

He raised his head to find her holding a mug and looking at him with concern. At least it wasn't pity. He took the cup.

She put the mug she still held on the table nearby and said, "I'll be right back."

Laura Jo returned wearing the jacket he'd offered her the night they'd made the king cakes. Picking up the mug she'd left behind, she took the lounge next to him. They sat in silence for a long time.

Finally Laura Jo said, "Do you want to talk about it?"

"No."

She made no comment, as if she accepted it was a part of him that he wouldn't share. Something about her being willing to do that endeared her even more to him and made him want to have her understand. "You asked me a few days ago about Mike being in an accident, remember?"

He didn't see her nod but somehow he knew she had.

"It was a night like tonight. Clear and warm for the time of the year. I had this great idea that we'd drive to the beach after the dance was over. After all, I'd be leaving in a few days for Birmingham to do my fellowship. My girlfriend, who was the queen that year, was having her last hoorah with her friends, so why not? Mike was going to ride with me and some of the other guys were going to meet us down there."

He swiped his fingers through his hair.

"I'd had a few drinks but I'd been so busy being king I'd had little time to eat, let alone drink. Mike, on the other hand, had had too much. I told him more than once to buckle his seat belt. But he wouldn't listen. I was feeling wild and free that night. I knew I was going too fast for the road… Long story short, I ran off the road, pulled the car back on and went off the other shoulder. And the car rolled. I was hardly injured. Mike was thrown out. It broke his back."

"Oh, Mark."

He jumped up and started pacing. "I don't want your pity. I don't deserve it." Thankfully, Laura Jo said nothing more. "That's not the worst of it." He spun and said the words that he was sure would turn her against him. "I left. The next day I packed my bags, gave up my residency in Birmingham and accepted one in California. I've only seen him a few times since I watched him being put into an ambulance." He all but spat the last sentence.

Mark stopped pacing and placed his back to Laura Jo, not wanting to see the disgust he feared was in her eyes. She made a small sound of anguish. He flinched. His spine stiffened and his hands formed balls at his side. He hung his head.

Laura Jo felt Mark's guilt and pain ripple through her like the sting of a whip. How quickly and effortlessly Mark had worked himself past her emotional barriers. She cared for him. Wanted to help him past the hurt.

No wonder he was so hypervigilant about people buckling up in his car. Now that she thought about it, he'd even hesitated when he'd had to drive someone in his car. He found the responsibility too weighty.

She went to him. Taking one of his fists, she kissed the top of his hand and began gently pulling his fingers open until she could thread her own between his. She leaned her head against his arm. "It wasn't your fault, even if you don't believe it."

Mark snorted. "And it wasn't my fault that I was such a lousy friend that I ran out on him when he needed me most. That was unforgivable. But that wasn't enough, I've compounded it by years of not really having anything to do with him. I was closer to Mike than I was to my own brother. How could I have done that to him? Even tonight I was a coward."

"You know, it's not too late," she said quietly. "You're the one who has been telling me that."

"It's way past too late. How do I tell him I'm sorry I put him in a wheelchair while I still walk around?"

Laura Jo heard his disgust for himself in his voice.

"The same way I have to forgive my parents for the way they treated me. We have to believe people can change and grow."

He took her in his arms and looked down at her. "It's easy for someone with a heart as big as yours to forgive. Not everyone can or will do that."

His lips found hers.

Mark didn't ask for entrance. She greeted him. Welcomed his need. Her hands went to his shoulders. She massaged the tension from them before her fingers moved up his neck into his hair.

His desperation to lose himself in her goodness made him kiss her more deeply. She took all he gave with no complaint. There was a restlessness to his need, as if he was looking for solace. He pulled her closer, gathering her dress as he did so.

For tonight she could be that peaceful place if that was what he needed. Laura Jo tightened her arms around his neck and returned his kiss.

"I need you," he groaned. His lips made a trail down her neck.

Brushing her dress away, he dropped a kiss on the ridge of her shoulder. His tongue tasted her. The warm dampness he left behind made her quake. His other hand slipped under the edge of the back of her dress and roamed, leaving a hot path of awareness.

"And I need you," she whispered against his ear.

Mark pushed her dress farther down her arm. His lips followed the route of the material, leaving hot points along her skin. Laura Jo furrowed her fingers through his hair, enjoying the feel of the curl between her fingers.

He released the hook at the back of her neck and her dress hung at her elbows. Her breasts tingled with anticipation. His head lowered to kiss the top of one breast. He pushed the edge of her dress away from her nipple and took it into his mouth and tugged lightly. She shivered from the sensation. His tongue circled and teased her nipple until she moaned into the evening air.

When his mouth moved to the other breast he cupped the first one. The pad of his thumb found the tip of her nipple and caressed it. He circled her nipple with the end of his index finger until it stood at attention. He lifted the mound and placed a kiss on it.

Her heated blood rushed to her center and pooled there. She wanted to see and feel as much of Mark as he was of her. Her hands found his lapels and slid beneath them to his hard chest. There she worked his coat off. She wanted to touch him. Feel his skin. This had gone beyond giving comfort to a desire that was building into a powerful animal. It had been feeding and waiting since the first time Mark had touched her. The more she knew about him, saw him, felt his kindness, that longing had grown. Now there was no denying it or fighting it.

Mark's lips came back to hers as he shook himself out of his tux jacket and let it fall down his arms. Laura Jo's fingers went to the bow tie and released it, pulling it away and dropping it beside his jacket. His lips returned to her neck as Laura Jo removed first one stud and then another until she found his skin beneath his shirt.

The tip of her fingers lightly grazed the small patch of hair covering his warm skin. Yes, she'd found what she was looking for.

As Mark's mouth moved to hers for a hot, sinuous kiss, she yanked at his shirt, removing it from his pants. She wrapped her arms around his waist then she ran her hands over his back. She enjoyed the ripple of his muscles as they reacted to her touch. Would she ever get enough of touching him?

Mark gathered her dress, bringing it up until he could put his hand on her thigh. His fingers made circular motions along her bare skin. Slowly, his hand slid higher and higher until he ran his finger over the barrier of her panties at her core.

Laura Jo involuntarily flexed toward him. She'd

never wanted a man to touch her more than she did at that moment.

With a growl of frustration, he set her on her feet. "I hope I don't live to regret this." He kissed her on the forehead. "Promise me you'll stay right here."

With heart pounding and body tight with need, Mark hurried into the house and scooped up the bedding in the extra bedroom. He grabbed two pillows, as well. With long strides, he walked back through the house. When he exited he was relieved to find Laura Jo waiting for him right where he'd left her. She had pulled her dress straps up over her shoulders. That was fine. He'd soon be removing her dress completely.

"What?" she murmured, as he came out of the house with his load.

"I want to see you under the stars."

He flipped the heavy spread out, not taking the time to make it neat. He lay down on his side and stretched out a hand in invitation for her to join him. His heart went to drumroll pace when she put her hand in his. This amazing woman was accepting him, even with all she'd learned about him.

She lifted her dress, giving him a tantalizing glimpse of her leg as she came to her knees before him.

Letting go of her hand, he used his finger to run a caressing line down her arm from her shoulder to her elbow. There he circled, then went to her wrist. He was encouraged by the slight tremble of her hand when he took it and eased her closer.

"Kiss me."

She leaned into him, pressing her lips against his. His hand pulled at her dress, bringing it up her leg. Gliding his hand underneath, he ran it along her thigh, moving to the inside then out again.

Laura Jo deepened their kiss.

His finger found the bottom of her panty line and followed it around to the back of her leg then forward again. She placed small kisses across his forehead and then nipped at his ear. He captured her gaze and watched her eyes widen as he slid a finger beneath her underwear at her hip. She gasped as his finger brushed her curls. He moved his finger farther toward her center and found wet, hot heat. His length strained to find release. She moaned against his mouth and bucked against his finger as he entered her.

"Mark." She drew his name out like a sound of adoration as she put her head back and closed her eyes.

When her hand grazed his straining length behind his zipper he jerked. The woman had him aroused to a painful point. The raw need that had built in him sought release. He feared he might lose his control and be like a teen in the backseat of a car as he fumbled to have all he dreamed of. Laura Jo ran her life with a tight rein and here she was exposing herself completely to him. That knowledge only increased his wish to give her pleasure.

"If you continue that I'm not going to be responsible for what I do," he growled. When had he been more turned on?

Laura Jo felt the same way. It had been a long time for her but she couldn't remember this gnawing hunger for another person that begged for freedom. She wanted to crawl inside Mark, be surrounded by him and find the safety and security she'd been missing for so many years.

He removed his finger.

She made a sound of protest.

"You have too many clothes on."

Could she be so bold as to remove her dress in front of him? She was thankful for the dim light. She was no longer a maiden. She'd had a child, gained a few mature pounds and things on her body had moved around. Would Mark be disappointed?

"Sit up on your knees, Laura Jo," he coached, as he moved to a sitting position.

Laura Jo did as he asked. As he gathered the fabric of her dress she shifted, releasing the long length of material from behind her knees. With it in rolls at her waist, he said, "Raise your arms."

She did so and he slipped the dress off over her head. Braless, she was exposed to Mark and the elements, except for her tiny panties. The cool air of the night licked her body, making her shudder. She was thankful for it because it covered her nervousness. She crossed her arms over her breasts.

"Please, don't hide from me," Mark said in a

guttural tone filled with emotion. "You're beautiful. I want to admire you in the moonlight."

She'd been so absorbed in him she hadn't noticed there was a full moon. Slowly, very slowly, she let her hands fall to her sides. Mark's look started at the apex of her legs and traveled upward. He paused at her breasts. They were already prickly with awareness and had grown heavy. She looked down to see her nipples standing ridged from the cool air and Mark's hot gaze.

He cupped both breasts and she quivered.

"So responsive," he murmured, more to himself than to her. "Lie down. I want to touch all of you."

"But you still have all your clothes on," she protested.

He chuckled dryly. "If I don't remain dressed I might not be able to control myself."

"But I want to—"

"Later. Now I want to give you pleasure."

He nudged her shoulder then supported her until she lay on her back.

Laura Jo felt exposed, a wanton. She shuddered.

"I'm sorry, you must be cold." He leaned behind him and brought a blanket over them. "I hate to cover up all this beauty but maybe next time..."

Would there be a next time? Did she want more?

He rested his hand on the center of her stomach. Her breathing was erratic and shallow. He kissed the hollow of her shoulder. She pushed his open shirt off his shoulders. He finished removing it and threw it over his shoulder to the deck.

Her hand went to the nape of his neck. "I want to feel your skin touching mine."

"Ah, sweetheart..." Mark kissed her gently and brought her against his warm, inviting chest.

Laura Jo went from shivering to feeling warm and sheltered in the harbor of Mark's arms.

Mark lay down, bringing her with him. His mouth found hers. One of his hands went to her waist and shimmered over the curve of her hip and down her thigh and back up to cup her breast.

Her hands found his chest. She took her time discovering the rises and falls as she appreciated the breadth of his muscles as her hand traveled across his skin. Her palm hovered over the meadow of hair, enjoying the springiness of it.

He sucked in a breath.

She let her hand glide downward along his ribs and lower. He groaned when she brushed the tip of his manhood. With that he flipped the blanket off, letting it fall over her. In one smooth, agile movement he stood. He sat in the closest chair and proceeded to remove his socks and shoes. Seconds later his pants found the deck. He looked like a warrior of old as he stood with his feet apart, his shaft straight, with the moonlight gleaming off the water behind him.

Laura Jo bit her lower lip. This piece of masculine beauty was all hers for tonight.

She pushed away the blanket and opened her arms. Mark opened a package and covered his manhood then came down to her. She pulled the cover over them.

His fingers looped into the lace band of her panties and tugged them off. She kicked her feet to finish the process.

"Perfect," Mark murmured, as he kissed the shell of her ear and his fingers traveled over the curve of her hip. "I want you so much."

Desire carried every word. She was wanted. Mark showed her in every way that she was desired by him. It fed her confidence. She arched her neck as his mouth traveled downward to the hollow beneath her chin, to the curve of a breast and out to her nipple. His hand went lower, where it tested and teased until she flexed.

Her core throbbed, waiting, waiting...

He slid a finger inside her, found that spot of pleasure and she bucked.

"So hot for me," he ground out, before placing a kiss on her stomach.

Mark said it as if he didn't think she could want him. Was the guilt he carried that heavy?

Laura Jo pushed him to his back. He made a sound of complaint. She slid on top of him and poured all she felt into making him feel desired. Positioning herself so that his tip was at her entrance, she looked into his eyes. Did he know how special he was to her? She pushed back and slowly took him inside her. His hands ran up and down her sides as his gaze bored into hers. She lifted and went down again.

Before she knew what had happened, Mark rolled her to her back and entered her with one bold thrust. His hold eased. "Did I hurt you?"

His question carried an anxiousness that went soul deep.

"No, you would never hurt me."

He wrapped his arms around her as if he never wanted to let her go. When he did let her go he rose on his hands and pulled out of her to push in again.

She moaned with pleasure and his movements became more hurried. Her core tightened, twisted until it sprang her into the heavens.

A couple of thrusts later, Mark groaned his release to the starry night and lay on her.

Just before his weight became too much he rolled to his side and gathered her to him, twining his legs with hers. He adjusted the blanket around them.

"Perfect," he said, worshipful praise, before brushing a kiss over her temple.

Mark woke to the sound of thunder rolling in the distance. Laura Jo was warm and soft next to him. He shifted. Hard boards weren't his normal sleeping choice but with Laura Jo beside him it wasn't so difficult. He would have some aches in the morning but it would be more than worth it.

He moved to lie on his back. As if she couldn't be parted from him, she rolled in his direction and rested her head on his shoulder. She snuggled close. What would it be like to have Laura Jo in his life all the time?

Lightning flashed in the clouds. Thunder rumbled.

A hand moved over his chest. His body reacted far too quickly for his comfort. Could he ever get enough of her?

"What're you thinking?"

He tightened his hold and then released it. "That if we don't go inside we're going to get wet." The first large drops of rain hit the porch.

"I'll get the pillows. You get the blankets," she said, jumping up. He followed.

They scooped up the bedding and ran to the door, making it inside just before the downpour started. They laughed at their luck. They stood watching the storm for a few seconds.

"Oh, we didn't get our clothes." Laura Jo moved to open the door.

Mark grabbed her hand. "Forget them.

He dropped the blankets on the floor. "Leave the pillows here."

"Where're we going?" Laura Jo asked.

He gave her a meaningful look. "Like you don't know?"

When she only dropped one pillow he raised a questioning brow.

"I'm not used to walking around the house in the nude and certainly not with a man."

Mark chuckled. "I'm glad to hear that. But you have a beautiful body. You shouldn't be so self-conscious."

"Not everyone has thought that."

Her tone told him that she wasn't fishing for a compliment. Had her ex said differently? "Trust me, you're the sexiest woman I've ever seen. Come with me and I'll show you just how much."

She hesitated.

"You can bring the pillow."

Taking her hand, he led her to his bedroom. He was glad that he'd pulled the covers off his guest-room bed instead of his own. Something told him that if he gave Laura Jo more than a couple of seconds to think she'd be dressing and asking to go home.

Mark didn't want that. He made a point not to spend all night with the women he dated because he didn't want them to get any idea that there would ever be anything permanent between them. But he wanted Laura Jo beside him when he woke in the morning. He wanted her close until he had to let her go. For her own good, he would have to let her go.

He clicked on the lamp that was on the table beside his bed. Pulling the covers back, he climbed in, and turned to look at Laura Jo. "You have to let go of that pillow sometime."

There was a moment or two of panic that she wouldn't, before she slowly dropped it.

His breath caught. She'd looked amazing in the moonlight, but in the brighter light she was magnificent. Her husband had really done a number on her to make her believe she wasn't wanted. Mark sure wanted her more than ever.

"Move over."

He grinned. Laura Jo had gained some confidence. She found her place beside him. Where she belonged. But his feeling of ultimate pleasure quickly moved to the deepest depths of despair. He couldn't keep her.

Laura Jo gave him a look of concern that soon

turned to one of insecurity. She slid her legs to the side of the bed.

"Oh, no, you don't. I'm not done with you." *Ever.* He rolled her to her back and kissed her.

Over the next minutes he teased, touched and tasted her body until he had her shaking beneath him. When he paused at her entrance she made a noise of disapproval. She wrapped her legs around his waist and urged him closer. He entered her and was lost forever.

Laura Jo woke up snuggled against Mark's hard body. She'd once thought he had none of the qualities in the man that she was looking for. She'd been so wrong. He had them all and more.

He was the opposite of Phil. When she had needed Mark to come help her at the shelter, he hadn't questioned it, just asked directions. He was good with Allie and she loved him. There had never been a question that he supported her cause with the shelter. He'd even been understanding about her relationship with her parents. He had been the support she hadn't had since she'd left her parents' home. Mark had become a person she could depend on, trust.

Her experiences with lovemaking had been about the other person doing all the receiving but Mark's loving had been all about giving, making sure she felt cherished. And she had.

She shifted until she could look at his face. His golden lashes tipped in brown lay unmoving against his skin. She resisted running her finger along the ridge of his nose. His strong, square jaw had a reddish tint of stubble covering it. She'd never seen a more handsome male in her life.

Her breath jerked to a stop. Oh, she couldn't be. But she was in love with Mark Clayborn!

"You're staring at me."

Her gaze jerked to his twinkling eyes. Could he see how she felt? Could she take a chance on trusting another man? She had Allie to consider. Had to act as if nothing had changed between them when everything had. In her best teasing tone she said, "You're so vain."

He moved to face her, propping his head on his hand. "That may be so but I did see you looking at me."

"So what if I was?" she asked in a challenging tone.

"Then..." he leaned into her "...I like it."

Putting an arm around her waist, he pulled her to him. His intention stood rock-hard ready between them. While he kissed her deeply, he positioned her above him and they became one.

CHAPTER EIGHT

AN HOUR LATER they were in the kitchen, working together to make breakfast. Laura Jo wore one of Mark's shirts while her dress hung on a deck chair, dripping, with Mark's jacket on another.

"I can't go home dressed in my evening gown," she mused, more to herself than to Mark.

"I'll find something around here that you can wear. Actually, I kind of like you in my shirt." He gave her a wolfish grin.

Warmth like the beach on a sunny day went through her. It was nice to be desired. It had been so long.

Wearing Mark's clothes and turning up in the morning instead of late at night in her evening gown was more than she wanted to explain to any of her neighbors. Allie deserved a mother who set a good example. More than that, she owed it to her not to become too involved with a man who wasn't planning to stay for the long haul.

Mark had once said that marriage wasn't part of their relationship. Had that changed after last night? He'd said he wanted nothing serious. She had major responsibilities, which always meant some level of permanency. Either way, she had other issues to handle in the next few days. She would face that later.

"Butter on your toast?" Mark asked, as he pulled two slices out of the toaster.

"Yes, please." Waking up with Mark, and spending the morning doing something as domestic as making a meal, felt comfortable, right. Did he sense it, too? She liked it that he didn't expect her to prepare their breakfast. Instead, it was a partnership.

A few minutes later they sat across from each other at the table, eating. Mark wore a pair of sport shorts and nothing else. He hadn't shaved yet and the stubble covering his jaw was so sexy she was having trouble concentrating on her food.

"Do you have to work today?" Mark asked.

"No. I work tomorrow morning. But I have to go to the shelter, see Mr. Washington." She couldn't keep from grinning. "And pick up Allie and Jeremy from school."

"I have to work from noon to eight. Could we maybe have a late dinner?"

"Eight is Allie's bedtime. And it's a school night."

He hesitated, stopping his fork halfway to his mouth. Was he thinking about all that was involved in seeing her? She and Allie were a package and she wanted to remind him of that.

"What's your schedule for Thursday night?"

"Work morning then I have to see Mr. Washington's friend then Mr. McClure about their donations."

"That's right. You're supposed to get the house on Friday. We'll make it a celebration. Take Allie to someplace fun."

"That sounds doable. By the way, I don't think I said thank you for all your help with the shelter. We couldn't have done it without you. You're a good man, Mark Clayborn."

A flicker of denial came to his eyes before it changed to something she couldn't name. He smiled. "Thank you for that, Laura Jo Akins. I think you believe it."

"And I think you should, too."

* * *

Mark had picked up his phone to call Laura Jo at least ten times over the course of the day. After returning her home, wearing a beach dress his sister-in-law had left there and one of his sweatshirts that had swallowed her whole, he had headed to work. He couldn't remember a more enjoyable morning. Laura Jo had just looked right in his kitchen. She was right for his life. The simple task of getting ready to leave for work, which turned out to include a very long shared shower, had been nicer when done with Laura Jo. He had it bad for her.

He picked up his phone. This time he texted her: How did it go with Mr. Washington?

Seconds later she returned, Good. Leaving now.

How like Laura Jo to say no more than necessary.

Unable to help himself, he typed, Looking forward to tomorrow evening.

She sent back a smiley face. He grinned. They had come a long way from the snarl that she had given him when they'd first met.

The next day, when he came out of one of the clinic examination rooms, he was told by the receptionist that there was a call for him. Was it Laura Jo? Was something wrong? His heart sank. Had she changed her mind about tonight? Mercy, he was starting to act lovesick.

"This is Dr. Clayborn."

"Hi, this is Marsha Gilstrap. Laura Jo's friend."

"Yes, I know who you are. Jeremy's mother."

"I'm calling because Laura Jo and I are getting ready to meet with the city about the shelter house. They have notified us at the last minute that they expect us to bring in the names of our board members. It has been only Laura Jo and I. Long story short, would you be willing to serve on our board? It would be for two years, with bi-monthly meetings. Would you be willing to serve?" Once again Marsha was talking like a whirlwind.

"Sure. Just let me know when and where I need to be." The shelter was a good cause and he would help Laura Jo in any way he could.

"Thanks, Dr. Clayborn."

"I thought we agreed to Mark."

"Thanks, Mark." With that she hung up.

That evening Mark drove straight from work to Laura Jo's apartment. He was looking forward to the evening far more than he should have been. Getting in too deep with Laura Jo could be disastrous. He wouldn't stay around forever and Laura Jo would expect that. But he couldn't help himself. He was drawn to her like no other woman he'd ever met.

Allie opened the door after he knocked.

"Hi, there." He went in and closed the door behind him. "Now that Mardi Gras is over, what do we need to look forward to next?"

"The Easter bunny bringing a large chocolate egg."

Mark nodded in thought. "Well, that does sound like something worth waiting for. Will you share yours with me?"

"Sure."

Laura Jo came up the hall. She wore nothing but a simple collared shirt that buttoned down the front and slacks but he still couldn't take his eyes off her. "Hello."

"Hi," she said, shyly for her.

He had gotten to her. She must be feeling unsure about them after the amount of time that had passed since they'd been together.

"Allie, would you do me a favor?"

She nodded.

"I'm thirsty. Would you get me a glass of water?"

As soon as she was out of sight Mark pulled Laura Jo to him. "What I'm really thirsty for is you." His mouth found hers.

Laura Jo had to admit that Mark had done well in choosing a place that would suit for a celebration and one Allie would enjoy. The pizza place was perfect. He'd even provided Allie with a handful of tokens so she could play games. Laura Jo was reasonably sure that this wasn't his usual choice of restaurant for a date.

"Thanks for bringing us here. Allie is having a blast." Laura Jo tried to speak loud enough to be heard over the cling and clang of the games being played and the overhead music.

"I love pizza, too," Mark said, as he brought a large slice of pepperoni to his mouth.

She liked his mouth, especially when it was on hers. His kiss at her door had her thinking of calling Marsha to see if Allie could spend the night then pulling Mark into her bedroom.

"So tell me what happened today about the

shelter," Mark said, after chewing and swallowing his bite.

"I collected all the donor money." She grinned. "They didn't remember but when I showed them each the promissory note with their signature on it, both men called their accounting departments and told them to cut a check."

Mark chuckled. "Mr. Washington knows his buddies well."

"The only glitch is that the bank keeps throwing these roadblocks in our way. Today's was that we had to show we have a full board. It couldn't just be Marsha and I."

"Did you know she called me?"

"She told me afterward that she had. I would have told her not to if she had asked."

"Why?"

"I didn't want to put you on the spot." After the other night she didn't want him to feel obligated because of their one night of passion.

"It's not a problem. Besides being extremely attracted to one of the board members, I do think the shelter is a worthy cause. I'm more than happy to serve on the board."

Allie came running up. "I need one more token to play a game."

Mark handed her a token. "After you play your game, I want you to play one with me."

"Okay," Allie said, all smiles.

"Stay where you can see me," Laura Jo reminded her, before Allie ran back to a nearby game.

Mark leaned in close so that he was speaking right into Laura Jo's ear. "Is there any chance for you and me to have some alone time?"

"You'll have to wait and see," Laura Jo said with a smile. "There's one more thing about the shelter I wanted to tell you. Just before you picked us up, Marsha called. The city has decided to take bids for the house. They know of no one else who's interested but they want everything to look aboveboard so they have to offer it out for bids."

"Sounds reasonable."

"Yeah, but what if someone comes in and outbids us?"

He looked at her and said in a serious tone, "Then you'll just have to raise the money or find somewhere else. You now have new board members you can depend on to help you make a decision. You and Marsha won't be all on your own anymore."

She smiled at him just as Allie returned. "I'm ready to play."

"Are you ready to lose because I'm the best whack-a-moler you've ever seen," Mark announced as he puffed out his chest.

Laura Jo and Allie laughed.

He really was fun to be around. "Famous last words, the saying goes, I think," Laura Jo remarked. It had just been Allie and herself for so long. Was she ready to share their life with Mark? She smiled. Maybe she was.

"Come on, young lady," Mark said, taking Allie's hand. "Let me show you."

They arrived back at Laura Jo's apartment, laughing at something Mark had done while trying to best Allie at the arcade game. When they had gotten into the car to leave the pizza place, he'd looked back at Allie and then turned to her. Laura Jo had placed her hand on the seat belt and said, "Thank you for seeing to our safety."

He gave her a wry smile before he started the car but he seemed less anxious.

"It's bath- and bedtime," Laura Jo told Allie as they entered her apartment. "Why don't you get your PJs and the water started? I'm going to fix some coffee for Mark and I'll be right in."

Allie left in the direction of her room and she and Mark went to the kitchen. She took the pot out of the coffee-maker and went to the sink.

Mark came up behind her and took the pot from her, setting it on the counter. "I'll fix the coffee while you see to Allie. Right now, I want a kiss." He turned her round and gathered her close, giving her a gentle but passionate kiss.

Laura Jo's knees went weak. Her arms went around him and she pulled him tight.

"Mama, I'm ready," Allie called.

Slowly Mark broke their connection. He brushed his hips against hers and grinned. "I am, too."

Laura Jo snickered and gave him a playful push. "I'll be back in a few minutes. Behave yourself while I'm gone."

Ten minutes later, Mark walked down the hall in the direction of Laura Jo's voice. He stopped and stood in the doorway of the room where the sound was coming from. The lights were off except for one small lamp with a fairy of some sort perched on top. Allie lay in bed and Laura Jo sat on the side, reading a book out loud. He leaned against the wall facing them and continued to listen. Allie's eyes were closed when Laura Jo shut the book and kissed her daughter on the forehead.

His heart constricted. What would it feel like to be a part of their inner circle?

Laura Jo looked at him and gave him a soft smile. She raised her hand and beckoned him to join her.

His heart beat faster. This was his invitation to find out. But if he took that step he'd be lost forever. He couldn't take on the responsibility of protecting them. What if he failed them, like he had Mike? No, as much as it would kill him to do so, he couldn't tangle their lives up in his. He'd let them down. Hurt them, disappoint them at best. They'd both had enough of that in their lives.

Laura Jo's smile faded. He backed out of the door, walked to the kitchen and sat at the small table.

* * *

What had just happened? Didn't Mark recognize that she'd just offered her life and heart to him? He'd turned it down. Flat.

Laura Jo could no longer pretend this was a casual thing between them. She couldn't afford to invest any of her life or Allie's in someone who was afraid of their ability to share a relationship. She needed a confident man during the good as well as the tough times. Mark didn't believe he was capable of being that man.

Even if she believed in him and convinced him they could make it, Mark had to believe in himself. She couldn't take the chance of Allie experiencing that loss and devastation, the almost physical pain of believing no one wanted her, if Mark decided he couldn't do it. Allie wouldn't be made to feel as if she were a piece of trash being tossed out the window of a car. No, she wouldn't let it happen. Wouldn't go through that again.

She had to break it off before they became any more involved. Her heartache she would deal with, but her daughter's heart she would protect. Maybe with time, and many tears during the night, she would get over Mark.

Laura Jo found him a few minutes later, looking at his coffee cup as he ran a finger around the edge. She poured herself a cup of coffee she had no intention of drinking and took the chair across the table from him.

"This isn't going to work, Mark."

"Why?"

"Because I need someone who'll be committed to the long haul. I deserve your wholehearted love and loyalty. I won't risk my heart or Allie's for anything less. That is the very least I will agree to."

"You know I won't take the chance. What if I can't do it? I won't hurt you. I'm no better than your ex-husband. When things get too tough to face, I'll be gone. Just like him. I've done it before. I'll do it again."

"You're still punishing yourself for something that isn't your fault. Mike's in a wheelchair because of a choice that he made, not you. Your way of atoning is to remain uninvolved emotionally with anyone you might feel something real for. That translates into a wife and family for you. I can see that you care about Allie and I think you care about me, too. I've spent a long time not trusting my judgment about men. You got past that wall. You're a better man than you give yourself credit for."

He didn't look at her. Her heart ached for him but she had to get through to him. Make him start really living again. He deserved it. She loved him enough to do that and send him away if she had to.

"You can't create someone else's happiness by being unhappy. You can't fix what happened to Mike. Even if you had been wrong. What you can do now is try to be a better friend than you were back then.

"The problem is you have run from and hidden from the issue too long. You've left the subject alone so long that it has grown and festered to a point it's out of control in your mind. Based on what I saw from Mike the other night, he feels no animosity toward you. To me it sounded as if he just misses his friend. Face it, clean the ugliness away then you can see yourself for the person you are. Good, kind, loving, protective and caring. It's time for you to like yourself.

"I hope that one day you realize that and find

someone to share your life with. It can't be Allie and I." Those last words almost killed her to say.

His chair scraped across the floor as he pushed it away from the table. He pinned her with a pointed look. His eyes were dark with sadness and something else. Anger? "Are you through?"

She nodded. She was sure she wasn't going to like what came next.

"I have issues, but you do, too. You carry a chip on your shoulder, Laura Jo. In the past nine years you have finished school on your own, raised a wonderful, happy child and started and helped to run a shelter for women, but still you feel you need to prove yourself to the world. You don't need your father and mother's or anyone else's approval. It's time to quit being that girl who had to show everyone she could do it by herself.

"You let your ex overshadow your life to the point it took me using a sledgehammer to get past your barriers. Laura Jo, not every guy is a jerk and doesn't face up to their responsibilities."

"Like you have?"

Mark flinched. She'd cut him to the core. But she had to get through to him somehow.

"I think I'd better go." He stood and started toward the door.

Shocked at his abrupt statement, she said, "I think it's for the best. Goodbye, Mark."

CHAPTER NINE

THE ONLY TIME Laura Jo could remember feeling so miserable had been when she'd taken Allie home from the hospital, knowing the child would have no father or grandparents to greet her. The pain had been heartbreakingly deep. She'd believed the scar had been covered over enough that she would never return to those emotions. But she'd been wrong.

They had rushed in all over again when Mark had walked out the door. The overwhelming despair was back. The problem this time was that it was even more devastating.

Looking back, she could see her goal when she'd been nineteen had been more about breaking away from her parents, standing on her own two feet and discovering what she believed in, instead of following their dictates. Turned out she'd let pride stand in her way all these years. It hadn't been fair to Allie, her parents or herself.

She appreciated Mark's fears, even understood where they came from, but she couldn't accept anything less than full commitment. Allie deserved that, and even she wouldn't settle for anything less.

Experience had shown her what it was like to have a man in her life who didn't stay around. She refused to put Allie through that. If she felt this awful about Mark leaving after they had known each other for such a short time, what would it have been like if they had been together longer?

The past had told her that the only way to survive disappointment and heartache, and in this case heartbreak, was to keep moving. It was Monday morning and Allie had school, she had to work.

Was Mark working the early shift? Moving around his big kitchen dressed only in his shorts? With them hung low on his hips? Bare-chested?

He'd called a couple of times but she had let the answering machine get it. If she spoke to him it would be too easy to open the door wide for him to come into her life. She just couldn't do that.

She groaned, afraid there would be no getting over Mark. She needed to stay busy, spend less time thinking about him. Forcing herself to climb out of bed, Laura Jo dressed for the day, making sure to have Allie to school on time.

Allie asked her during breakfast, "Why're you so sad, Mama?"

Laura Jo put on a bright smile and said in the most convincing voice she could muster, "I'm not sad. Why would I be sad?"

Allie gave her a disbelieving look but said nothing more. For that Laura Jo was grateful. She worried that she'd break down in tears in front of her daughter.

At midmorning, after just releasing a patient home from the ER, Laura's cell phone buzzed. Looking at it, she saw it was Marsha calling. It was unusual for her to call while Laura Jo was working. Something must have happened with the shelter.

"Hello. What's going on?"

"Someone has bid against us for the house. It's far over what we have and I don't see any way for us to come up with that amount of money."

Marsha told Laura Jo the figure. They were doomed. The new house wasn't going to happen this time. "You're right."

"What we'll have to do is use the money we do have to refurbish the place we're in now and start looking for another place to buy. Sorry my call was bad news."

"Me, too, but I was afraid this might happen when the city opened it for bids. I'd prepared myself for it. We'll start making plans this evening when I get home."

Laura Jo hung up. The sting had been taken out of the loss of the house by the loss of Mark. With him no longer in her life, it made everything else feel less important. She and Marsha would deal with this setback somehow.

A week later, her heart was still as heavy as ever over Mark. If she could just stop thinking about him and, worse, dreaming of him, she could start to heal. But nothing she did except working on the shelter, seemed to ease the continuous ache in her chest.

She and Marsha had just finished meeting with a contractor about ideas for changes at the shelter when Laura Jo was called to the front. There a man dressed in a suit waited.

"Can I help you?" she asked.

"Are you Laura Jo Akins?" The man said in an official manner.

"Yes."

"I was instructed to personally deliver this to you."

He handed her an official-looking envelope. Was this some sort of summons?

Laura Jo started opening the letter and before she could finish the man left. What was going on?

Printed on the front was a name of a lawyer's office. Why would a lawyer be contacting her? She opened the envelope and scanned the contents. Her heart soared and her mouth dropped open in disbelief. She thought of telling Mark first, but he wasn't in her life anymore.

"Marsha!" she yelled.

Her friend hurried down the hallway toward Laura Jo. "What's wrong?"

She waved the letter in the air. "You're never going to believe this. My father has bought the house the city was selling and he has deeded it over to me!"

That night Laura Jo wondered about her parents' generosity. Had they had a change of heart years ago but she wouldn't let them close enough to say so? She had been surprised at the krewe dance to discover they knew some of what had been going on in her life. Had they been watching over her? There had been that school scholarship that she'd been awarded that she'd had no idea she'd qualified for, which had covered most of her expenses. Had that been her parents' doing?

She'd told Mark that people had the capacity to change. Had her parents? After speaking to them, she'd certainly seen them in a different light. She'd also told Mark that people could forgive. Maybe it was past time she did.

On Saturday afternoon, Laura Jo pulled her car into the drive of her parents' home. Allie sat in the seat next to her. Laura Jo had told her about her grandparents a few days before. She had asked Allie to forgive her for not telling her sooner, and had also told Allie that they would be going to visit her grandparents on Saturday. Later that evening, Laura Jo had called the number that she'd known from childhood. Her mother had answered on the second ring. Their conversation had been a short one but during it Laura Jo had asked if she could bring Allie to meet them.

"Mama, what're we doing?" Allie asked.

"I'm just looking, honey. I used to live here." That was true but mostly she was trying to find the nerve to go further. The last time she'd been there, hurtful words had been spoken that had lasted for years.

A few minutes later, she and Allie stood hand in hand in front of her parents' front door. Allie rang the doorbell. Her mother must have been watching for them because the door was almost immediately opened by her mother herself. Not one of the maids. Her father was coming up the hall behind her.

"Hello, Laura Jo. Thank you for coming." Her mother sounded sincere.

"Mother and Daddy, this is Allie."

Her mother leaned over so that she was closer to Allie's level and smiled. "Hi, Allie. It's so nice to meet you."

Her father took the same posture. "Hello."

Allie stepped closer to Laura Jo. She placed a hand at Allie's back and said, "These are your grandparents."

Both her parents stood and stepped back.

Her mother said in a nervous voice Laura Jo had never heard, "Come in."

It felt odd to step into her parents' home after so much time. Little had changed. Instead of being led into the formal living room, as Laura Jo had expected, her mother took them to the kitchen. "I thought Allie might like to have some ice cream."

Allie looked at Laura Jo. "May I?"

"Sure, honey."

"Why don't we all have a bowl?" her father suggested.

When they were finished with their bowls of ice cream her mother asked Allie if she would like to go upstairs to see the room where Laura Jo used to sleep. Allie agreed.

Laura Jo looked at her father. "I don't know how to say thank you enough for your gift."

"We had heard that you were looking for support to buy it."

She should have known it would get back to them about why she'd been at the dance.

"It's a good cause and we wanted to help. Since we weren't there for you, maybe we can help other girls in the same position. I know it doesn't make up for the struggle you had."

It didn't, but at least she better understood her parents now. She had to share some of the fault also. "All those calls I made to Mom—"

"We thought we were doing what was best. That if we cut you off then you would see that you needed us and come back."

"But you wouldn't talk to me." She didn't try to keep the hurt out of her voice.

"We realized we had been too hard on you when you stopped calling. I'm sorry, Laura Jo. We loved you. Feared for you, and just didn't know how to show it correctly."

"You saw to it that I got the nursing scholarship, didn't you?"

He nodded. "We knew by then that you wouldn't accept if we offered to send you to school."

"I wouldn't have. It wasn't until recently that I realized that sometimes what we believe when we're young isn't always the way things are. You were right about Phil. I'm sorry that I hurt you and Mom. Kept Allie from you."

"We understand. We're proud of you. We have kept an eye on you both. You've done well. You needed to do it the hard way, to go out on your own. It took us a while to see that." Her strong, unrelenting father went on, with a catch in his voice, "The only thing we couldn't live with was not having you in our lives and not knowing our granddaughter."

Moisture filled her eyes for all the hurt and wasted opportunities through the years on both sides. Laura Jo reached across the table and took her father's hand. Forgiveness was less about her and more about her parents. A gift she could give them. "You'll never be left out of our lives again, I promise."

Three weeks after the fact Mark still flinched when he thought of Laura Jo accusing him of being a jerk and not living up to his responsibilities. The plain-talking Laura Jo had returned with a vengeance when she'd lectured him.

She was right, he knew that, but he still couldn't bring himself to talk to Mike. That was the place he had to start. He'd spent over ten years not being able to face up to Mike and what had happened that night. Could he be a bigger hypocrite?

He'd looked down on Laura Jo's ex, taking a

holier-than-thou approach when he'd been running as fast and far as Phil had when the going had got tough.

Every night he spent away from Laura Jo made him crave her more. He wasn't sleeping. If he did, he dreamed of her. The pain at her loss was greater than any he'd ever experienced. Even after the accident. He wasn't able to live without her. He'd tried that and it wasn't working.

He'd tried to call her a couple of times but she hadn't picked up.

Mark thought about Laura Jo's words. Didn't he want a family badly enough to make a change? Want to have someone special in his life? More importantly, be a part of Laura Jo's and Allie's world?

He'd been running for so long, making sure he didn't commit, he didn't know how to do anything else. It was time for it to stop. He had to face his demons in order to be worthy of a chance for a future with Laura Jo, if she would have him. How could he expect her to believe in him, trust him to be there for her, if he didn't believe it for himself? He had to get his own life in order before he asked for a permanent place in hers. And he desperately wanted that place.

Mark picked up the phone and dialed the number he'd called so many times he had it memorized by now. He'd been calling every day for a week and had been told that Mike wasn't available. Was he dodging Mark, as well?

He'd made his decision and wanted to act on it. It was just his luck he couldn't reach Mike. The devil of it was that he couldn't return to Laura Jo without talking to Mike first. She would accept nothing less. For his well-being as well as hers.

The day before, he'd received a call from Marsha. She'd told him how they had missed out on the house but then an anonymous donor had bought it outright and gifted it to them.

Mark was surprised and glad for Laura Jo. At least the dream she'd worked so hard for had come true. Marsha went on to say that she and Laura Jo no longer required a board but planned to have one anyway. Marsha wanted to know if he was still willing to serve on it.

"Have you discussed this with Laura Jo? She may not want me on it."

"She said that if you're willing to do it she could handle working with you on a business level. I think her exact words were, 'He's a good doctor and cares about people. I'm sure he'll be an asset.'"

Panic flowed through his veins. Laura Jo was already distancing herself from him. The longer it took to speak to Mike, the harder it would be to get her to listen.

Marsha said, "Look, Mark, I don't know what happened between you two but what I do know is that she's torn up about it. I love her like a sister and she's hurting. She can be hardheaded when it comes to the ones she loves. The only way to make her see reason is to push until she does."

"Thanks for letting me know."

The next day, when Mark had a break between patients, he tried Mike's number again. This time when a woman answered he insisted that he speak to Mike.

"Just a minute."

"Mark." Mike didn't sound pleased to hear from him.

"I was wondering if I could come by for a visit," Mark said, with more confidence than he felt.

"It will be a couple of days before I have time." Mike wasn't going to make this easy but, then, why should he. "I've been out of town and have some business I need to catch up on."

Mark wasn't tickled with having to wait, but he'd put it off this long so did two more days really matter?

"How does Thursday evening at seven sound?"

"I'll be here." Mike sounded more resigned to the idea than cheerful about the prospect. Mark couldn't blame him. His jaw tightened with tension from guilt and regret at the thought of facing him. He felt like a coward and had acted like one for years.

The next day an invitation arrived in the mail. It was to a garden party tea at the Herrons' mansion on Sunday afternoon. It was a fund-raiser for the new shelter. Had Laura Jo taken his advice and cleared the air with her parents? He looked forward to attending.

Two evenings later, Mark drove from Fairhope over the bay causeway to Mobile. Mike lived in one of the newer neighborhoods that Mark wasn't familiar with. He hadn't slept much the night before, anticipating the meeting with Mike, but, then, he hadn't slept well since the night he'd had Laura Jo in his arms. He drove up the street Mike had given as his address during their phone conversation. It was tree-lined and had well-cared-for homes. He pulled up alongside the curb in front of the number that Mike had given him. It was a yellow ranch-style home, with a white picket fence surrounding the front yard. Early spring flowers were just starting to show.

Mark sat for a minute. He'd prepared his speech. Had practiced and practiced what he was going to say, but it never seemed like enough. If Laura Jo were here, she would say to just share what was in his heart. To stop worrying. Taking a deep breath and letting it out slowly, he opened the car door and got out. Closing it, he walked around the car and up the walk.

He hadn't noticed when he'd pulled up that there were children's toys in the yard and near the front door. Mike had a child?

Mark winced when he saw the wheelchair ramp and hesitated before putting a foot on it to walk to the door. His nerves were as tight as bowstrings. He rang the doorbell. Seconds later, Tammy opened the door.

"Mark, how nice to see you again." She pulled the door wider. "Come on in. Mike's in the den with Johnny."

She closed the door and Mark followed her down an extrawide hall to a large room at the back of the house.

Mike sat in what could only be called the most high-tech of wheelchairs in the middle of the room. A boy of about three was handing him a block and together they were building a tower on a tray across Mike's knees. "Mark. Come on in. Let me introduce you to my son, Johnny."

Mark went over to Mike, who offered his hand for a shake. "Good to see you again."

Mike dumped the blocks into a bucket beside his chair and then set the tray next to it. "Come here, Johnny, I want you to meet someone."

At one time Mike would have introduced him as his best friend. By the way he acted he wasn't even a friend anymore.

The boy climbed into his father's lap and shyly curled into Mike. He looked up at Mark with an unsure gaze.

"Johnny," Mark said.

"I think it's is time for someone to go to bed."

Tammy reached out and took Johnny from Mike. "We'll let you two talk."

Mark watched them leave the room and turned back to Mike.

"I admire you."

"How's that?"

"Having a wife and family. The responsibility. How do you know you're getting it right?"

"Right? I have no idea that I am. I make the best decisions I can at the time and hope they are the correct ones. Tammy and I are partners. We make decisions together." Mike looked directly at him. "Everyone makes mistakes. We're all human and not perfect. We just have to try harder the next time."

Was that what he'd been doing? Letting a mistake color the rest of his life? If he couldn't be sure he'd be the perfect husband or father then he wouldn't even try.

Before Mark could say anything more, Mike said, "Take a seat and quit towering over me. You always made a big deal of being taller than me. Remember you used to say that was why you got the girls, because they saw you first in a crowd."

Mark gave halfhearted grin. Had Mike just made a joke?

Taking a seat on the edge of the sofa, Mark looked around the room.

"Why are you here, Mark? After all these years, you show up at my house now," Mike said, as he maneuvered his chair closer and into Mark's direct sight line.

He scooted back into the cushions. "Mike, I need to clear the air about a couple of things."

"It's well past time for that."

Those words didn't make Mark feel any better. "I'm embarrassed about how I acted after the accident. I'm so sorry I left without speaking to you and have done little to stay in touch since. Most of all, I'm sorry I put you in that damn chair." Mark looked at the floor, wall, anywhere but at Mike.

Moments passed and when Mike spoke he was closer to Mark than he had been before. "Hey, man, you didn't put me in this chair. I did. I was drunk and not listening to anything anyone said."

"But I was the one going too fast. I'd driven that part of the road a hundred times. I knew about that ninety-degree turn. I overcorrected." Mark looked up at him.

"You did. But I wouldn't have been thrown out if I'd worn my seat belt. I don't blame you for that. But I have to admit it hurt like hell not to have your support afterwards. I can't believe you did me that way."

Mark's stomach roiled as he looked at a spot on the floor. "I can't either. That isn't how friends should act." He looked directly at Mike. "All I can do is ask you to forgive me and let me try to make it up to you."

"If you promise not to run out on me again, and buy me a large steak, all will be forgiven."

Mark smiled for the first time. "That I can do."

"And I need a favor."

Mark sat forward. "Name it."

"I need a good general practice doctor to oversee an experimental treatment that I'm about to start. Do you know one?"

"I just might," Mark said with a grin. "What's going on?"

"I just returned from Houston, where they are doing some amazing things with spinal injuries. With all these guys coming back from war with spinal problems, what they can do has come a long way even from nine years ago. I will have a procedure done in a few weeks and when I return home I need to see a doctor every other day to check my site and do bloodwork. My GP is retiring and I'm looking for someone to replace him who Tammy can call day or night." He grinned. "She worries. Doesn't believe me when I tell her what the doctor has said. Likes to hear it from the doc himself."

"I'll be honored to take the job. I'll even make house calls if that will help."

"I may hold you to that."

For the next forty-five minutes, he and Mike talked about old times and what they were doing in their lives now. Mike had become a successful businessman. He had invented a part for a wheelchair that made it easier to maneuver the chair. As Mark drove away he looked back in his rearview mirror. Mike and Tammy were still under the porch light where he had left them. Tammy's hand rested on Mike's shoulder. That simple gesture let Mark know that Mike was loved and happy.

Mike had a home, a wife and child, was living

the life Mark had always hoped for but was afraid
to go after. All Mark owned was his car and Gus.
He'd let the one special person he wanted in his
life go. Ironically, Mike had moved on while he
had stayed still. And he had been the one feeling
sorry for Mike, when he had more in life than
Mark did. He wanted that happiness in his life
too and knew where to find it.

If he could get Laura Jo to listen. If she would
just let him try.

CHAPTER TEN

LAURA JO COULDN'T believe the difference a few
weeks had made in her life. It was funny how
she'd been going along, doing all the things she'd
always done, and, bam, her life was turned up-
side down by her daughter having a skinned
knee. She'd worked Mardi Gras parades before
but never had she had a more eventful or emotional season.

She scanned her parents' formal backyard garden. There were tables set up among the rhodo-
dendrons, azaleas and the dogwood trees. None
were in full bloom but the greenery alone was
beautiful. The different tables held canapés and
on one sat a spectacular tea urn on a stand that
swung with teacups surrounding it. People in
their Sunday best mingled, talking in groups. The
eye-popping cost to attend the event meant that
the shelter could double the number of women
they took in. Her parents had convinced her to

let them to do this fund-raiser so that she could get the maximum out of the grant. She'd agreed and her mother had taken over.

How ironic was it that she had rejected her parents and they were the very ones who were helping her achieve her dreams? Her anger and resentment had kept her away from her parents, not the other way around. Forgiveness lifted a burden off her and she was basking in the sunshine of having a family again. She only wished Mark could feel that way, as well. She still missed him desperately.

Allie's squeal of delight drew her attention. Laura Jo located her. She was running down the winding walk with her new dress flowing in her haste.

"Mark," she cried, and Laura Jo's stomach fluttered.

She'd thought he might be here, had prepared herself to see him again, but her breath still stuck in her throat and her heart beat too fast. Each day became harder without him, not easier.

Already she regretted agreeing to let him remain on the board. Now she would have to continue to face him but he was too good an advocate for the shelter to lose him. At least, that was what she told herself. Somehow she'd have to learn to deal with not letting her feelings show.

When Allie reached Mark he whisked her up into his arms and hugged her close. The picture was one of pure joy between them.

Laura Jo had worked hard not to snap at Allie when she'd continued to ask about where Mark was and why they didn't see him anymore. Finally, Laura Jo had told her he wouldn't be coming back and there had been tears on both sides.

Mark lowered Allie onto her feet and spoke to her. Allie turned and pointed in Laura Jo's direction. Mark's gaze found hers, even at that distance. Her heart flipped.

He started toward her.

A couple of people she'd known from her Mardi Gras court days joined her. They talked for a few minutes but all the while Laura Jo was aware of Mark moving nearer.

He stood behind her. She'd know anywhere that aftershave and the scent that could only be his. Her spine tingled.

As the couple moved away Mark said in a tone that was almost a caress, "Laura Jo."

She came close to throwing herself into his arms but she had to remain strong. She turned around, putting on her best smile like she'd been taught so many years ago. "Hello, Mark, glad you could come."

"I wouldn't have missed it."

His tone said that was the truth.

"Marsha told me that you got the house after all. That's wonderful. With the grant and all the money you've raised, you'll be able to furnish it."

"Yes. My father was the one to outbid us. He then gave it to me."

His brow wrinkled. "You were okay with that?"

"I was. The women needed it too badly for me to use my disagreement with my parents against them. It really was a gift to me anyway. He wanted to make amends by helping other women going through the same experience I had."

Mark nodded. "It sounds like you and your parents worked things out."

"I wouldn't say that it's all smooth going. But I've forgiven them. We're all better for that. They want to see their granddaughter and Allie needs them. I don't have the right to deny any of them that."

"Mama, look who's here," Allie said from beside her.

Laura Jo hadn't seen her approach, she'd been so absorbed in Mark. She turned. "Who—?"

Allie held Gus's leash. Behind the dog sat Mike and next to him stood his wife. She looked back at Mark.

He smiled and turned toward the group. "I brought a few friends with me. I hope you don't mind?"

Did this mean what she thought it did? Mark had taken what she'd said to heart and had gone to see his friend. "Hello, Mike and Tammy. Of course you're welcome. I'm glad to see you again."

"We're glad to be here. This is some event. And I understand it's for a very worthy cause. I think we'll have Allie show us where the food is." Mike winked at Mark. "We'll see you around, buddy."

Laura Jo looked between them, not sure what the interchange meant.

"You're busy. I think I'll get some food also." Mark captured her hand. "When this is over, can we talk?"

A lightning shock of awareness and a feeling

of rightness washed through her simultaneously. "It'll be late."

"I'll wait."

Mark sat in Mr. Herron's den, having a cup of coffee while he waited for Laura Jo. Her father was there, along with Allie and Gus. Mr. Herron had apparently noticed Mark was hanging around after the other guests were leaving and had taken pity on him by inviting him in for coffee and a more comfortable seat.

The longer Mark sat there the more nervous he became. Would Laura Jo listen to what he had to say? Would she believe that he had changed? Would she be willing to take a chance on him? He broke out in a sweat, just thinking about it.

She and her mother finally joined them. He stood. Laura Jo looked beautiful but tired. Had she been getting as little sleep as he had?

As if her mother knew Laura Jo needed some time alone with him, Mrs. Herron said, "Why don't you let Allie stay with us tonight? We can get her to school in the morning. She can wear the clothes she wore from home to here today."

"Is that okay with you, Allie?" Laura Jo asked.

"Yes. Can Gus stay, too?"

"I think you need to let your grandparents get used to having you before you start inviting Gus to stay," Mark said with a smile.

Ten minutes later, he and Laura Jo, with Gus in the backseat, were leaving her parents' house. She had touched her seat belt when he'd looked.

"Old habits are hard to break," he said in explanation.

"Not a bad habit to have," she assured him in a warm tone. That was one of the many things he loved about Laura Jo. She understood him.

"I hope you don't mind me taking Gus home. I don't want you to think I planned to lure you to my house. I just thought Allie would be glad to see him. I didn't think it all the way through."

"She was, and I don't mind riding to your house."

As they traveled through the tunnel Laura Jo remarked, "I've never known my parents to let a dog in the house."

"Gus does have that effect on people."

She went on as if more in thought than conversation, "Come to think of it, I've never seen my father invite another man into his private space."

"Maybe that's his way of giving me a seal of approval."

She pieced him with a look. "Are you asking for a seal of approval from my father?"

"No, the only seal of approval I'm looking for is from you."

She studied him for a minute before asking, "Are you going to tell me about Mike and Tammy or keep me in suspense?"

"It took me a while to admit you were right. Actually, I knew all along that you were. I just didn't want to admit it."

"So what made you decide to talk to Mike?" She had laid her head back and closed her eyes.

He hadn't planned to go into this as they traveled. But as usual Laura Jo had a way of surprising him. "Why don't you rest and I'll tell you when we get to my house?"

"Sounds like a plan."

By the time Mark pulled into his drive, Laura Jo was sleeping. Here he was, planning to bare his heart to her after weeks of being separated, and she'd fallen asleep. He let Gus out of the car and went to open the front door.

Going to Laura Jo's door, he opened it, unbuckled her and scooped her into his arms. She mumbled and wrapped her arms around his neck, letting her head rest on his chest. He kicked the passenger door closed and carried her inside.

He loved having her in his arms again. After pushing the front door closed, he went to his favorite chair and sat down. She continued to sleep and he was content just having her close.

Sometime later Laura Jo stirred. He placed a kiss on her temple and her eyelids fluttered open.

"Hello," she mumbled against his neck. Then she kissed him.

The thump-thump of his heart went to bump-bump.

Her lips touched the ridge of his chin, while a hand feathered through his hair near his ear.

His hopes soared. His manhood stirred. Had she missed him as much as he'd missed her? "Laura Jo, if you keep that up, talking is the last thing that will happen."

"So talk," she murmured, before her mouth found the corner of his. "I'm listening."

"Maybe we need to go out on the deck."

"Mmm, I like it here." She wiggled around so she could kiss him fully on the mouth.

His length hardened. If he didn't say what he needed to say now, he wouldn't be doing so for a long time.

"I can't believe that I'm doing this…" He pushed her away until he could see her face. She blinked at him and gave him a dreamy smile. "Why did you agree to talk to me? Was it because you saw me with Mike? You haven't answered any of my phone calls in the past few weeks."

"I hoped…"

"Hoped what? That I had changed my mind? Hoped you'd gotten through to me? Hoped there was a chance for us?"

"Yes," she whispered.

"Do you want there to be?"

By now she was sitting a little straighter and her eyes had turned serious. "Tell me what made you decide to go talk to Mike. When you left my place I didn't think you ever would."

"I went because I discovered that I was more afraid of something else than I was of facing Mike."

Her gaze locked with his. "What?"

"Losing any chance of ever having you in my life."

"Oh, Mark. I thought I had lost you forever until I saw you with Mike today. I knew then that you thought we had something worth fighting for. I've been so miserable without you." She took his face in her hands and kissed him.

"We've both been running from our pasts. I think it's time for us to run toward our future. Together."

His arms tightened around her. Their kiss deepened. He had to have her. Beneath him, beside him, under him. Forever.

Mark lifted her off him and she stood. He quickly exited the chair. Taking her hand, he led her to his bedroom. Putting his hands on her shoulders, he turned her around and unzipped her dress. Pushing it off and letting it fall to the floor, he kissed her shoulder.

"I've missed you so much it hurt."

"I felt the same."

He released her bra and it joined her dress. There was a hitch in her breathing when he cupped her breasts. She leaned back against him. As his hands roamed, she began to squirm.

She flipped around to face him. "I want you."

Her hands went to his waist and started releasing his belt.

"No more than I want you."

With them both undressed, they found the bed and the world that was theirs alone.

Sometime later, Mark lay with Laura Jo in his arms. Her hair tickled his nose but he didn't mind. All was right with his world if she was in it.

Laura Jo shifted, placed a hand in the center of his chest and looked up at him. "Hi, there."

He looked at her and smiled. "Hey, yourself."

For a few moments he enjoyed the feel of her in his arms before he said, "I've worked for years not to become emotionally involved with anyone. I didn't think I could trust myself. Then along came you and Allie. I've been miserable without you both. I've always wanted a family and when a wonderful one was offered to me, like an idiot I turned it down. I won't do that again if the invitation is still open. See, the problem is that I've fallen in love with you."

With moisture in her eyes Laura Jo stretched up and placed a kiss on his mouth. "I love you, too, but are you sure that's what you want? What you can live with? I can't take any chances. It has to be forever. Kids or no kids. Good or bad days. Sickness or health."

Mark leaned forward so that his face was only inches from hers. "Until death do us part."

"I can live with that."

Her kiss told him she meant it.

* * * * *

*Look out for Susan Carlisle's
next Medical Romance*™
HIS BEST FRIEND'S BABY
Available in December 2015
*Don't miss the next installment of the
fabulous* MIDWIVES ON-CALL *series!*

MILLS & BOON®
Large Print Medical

November

Always the Midwife	Alison Roberts
Midwife's Baby Bump	Susanne Hampton
A Kiss to Melt Her Heart	Emily Forbes
Tempted by Her Italian Surgeon	Louisa George
Daring to Date Her Ex	Annie Claydon
The One Man to Heal Her	Meredith Webber

December

Midwife...to Mum!	Sue MacKay
His Best Friend's Baby	Susan Carlisle
Italian Surgeon to the Stars	Melanie Milburne
Her Greek Doctor's Proposal	Robin Gianna
New York Doc to Blushing Bride	Janice Lynn
Still Married to Her Ex!	Lucy Clark

January

Unlocking Her Surgeon's Heart	Fiona Lowe
Her Playboy's Secret	Tina Beckett
The Doctor She Left Behind	Scarlet Wilson
Taming Her Navy Doc	Amy Ruttan
A Promise...to a Proposal?	Kate Hardy
Her Family for Keeps	Molly Evans

MILLS & BOON®
Large Print Medical

February

Hot Doc from Her Past	Tina Beckett
Surgeons, Rivals...Lovers	Amalie Berlin
Best Friend to Perfect Bride	Jennifer Taylor
Resisting Her Rebel Doc	Joanna Neil
A Baby to Bind Them	Susanne Hampton
Doctor...to Duchess?	Annie O'Neil

March

Falling at the Surgeon's Feet	Lucy Ryder
One Night in New York	Amy Ruttan
Daredevil, Doctor...Husband?	Alison Roberts
The Doctor She'd Never Forget	Annie Claydon
Reunited...in Paris!	Sue MacKay
French Fling to Forever	Karin Baine

April

The Baby of Their Dreams	Carol Marinelli
Falling for Her Reluctant Sheikh	Amalie Berlin
Hot-Shot Doc, Secret Dad	Lynne Marshall
Father for Her Newborn Baby	Lynne Marshall
Wedding Bells for the ER Doc?	Dianne Drake
Safe in the Surgeon's Arms	Molly Evans